SO-AHM-438

11.⁰⁰

Leïla Sebbar was born in Algeria to a French mother and an Algerian father, both teachers until Independence. She studied in Paris and has lived there for the last twenty years. She is a leading writer on Algerian feminist themes.

Dorothy S. Blair first became interested in literature in French from Africa in the 1950s. In addition to her own work of criticism, she has published translations of many books written in French by African writers, concentrating more recently on woman writers from the Mahgreb.

Sherazade

LEÏLA SEBBAR

Translated by Dorothy S. Blair

LIBRARY
FRANKLIN PIERCE COLLEGE
RINDGE, NH 03461

QUARTET BOOKS

PQ
2679
.E244
S5
1999

First published by Quartet Books Limited in 1991
A member of the Namara Group
27 Goodge Street
W1P 2LD

This edition published by Quartet Books Limited in 1999

Copyright © by Leïla Sebbar 1982
Translation and Introduction copyright © by Dorothy S. Blair 1991

First published in France by Editions Stock 1982 as *Shérazade, 17ans, brune, frisée, les yeux verts*

All rights reserved. No part of this book may be reproduced in any form or by any means without the prior written permission of the publisher

The moral right of Leïla Sebbar to be identified as author of this work has been asserted in accordance with the Copyright, Designs and Patents Act 1988

A catalogue record for this book is available from the British Library

ISBN 0 7043 8125 7

Printed and bound in Great Britain by Cox & Wyman, Reading, Berks

Glossary

Babylon, derogatory term used for the decadent Western capitals by immigrants, usually those from the West Indies

Beur, person of North African origin (Algerian, Moroccan, Tunisian), usually second-generation immigrant, born or having grown up in France. This word is *verlan* (backslang) for *Arabe*, as pronounced with strongly rolled R and voiced B by North Africans.

burnous, long, loose woollen cloak with hood

CAP, *Certificat d'Aptitude Professionnelle*, a technical diploma

DASS, *Département d'Action Sanitaire et Sociale*, Social Welfare Department

Eid, feast day, Muslim religious holiday

fouta, length of striped material worn by rural women of Maghreb round their waist, over their dress

haïk, veil, square of woollen cloth in which

women envelop themselves in North Africa when venturing out of doors

harissa, an extremely hot, spicy, red-pepper sauce

harki, Algerian who volunteered to fight in the French army against the forces of Resistance during the Algerian War; repatriated to France, they were called 'French Muslims'

IRCAM, *Institut de Recherche et de Coordination Acoustique-Musique* (Institute for Research and Coordination of Acoustic Music)

kanoun, a brazier

mechta, a hamlet

medresa, Qur'anic school

merguez, a hot, spicy sausage

moujahideen, partisans, fighting for Independence during the Algerian War

pied-noir, person of European origin who was born and lived in Algeria, but left during or after the Algerian War to settle in France

RER, *Réseau express régional*, suburban line linked to Paris Metro at Châtelet and Charles de Gaulle-Etoile

Roumiette, dim. fem. of *Roumi*, *Roumia* (f.), derogatory word applied by North Africans to French or other Europeans

Sonacotra, *Société Nationale de Construction de Logements pour Travailleurs*, by extention, the immigrant workers living in the blocks of sub-economic flats, built to house them

Sonatrac, *Société Nationale de Transport et de*

Commericialisation des Hydrocarbures, National Society for Transport and Marketing of Hydrocarbons

willaya, a Department in Algeria

ZUP, Zone à urbaniser en priorité, priority urban development area

Introduction

Leïla Sebbar was born in Algeria in 1941 in Aflou, a remote village on the High Plateaux, and grew up during the Algerian War of Independence in a rural area near Tlemcen where her parents – a French mother and Algerian father – were schoolteachers, like the parents of Julien Desrosiers in her novel, *Sherazade*. There are clearly autobiographical echoes of the author's family in the story told by one of the colleagues of Julien's father (cf. pp. 17–19).

Besides many novels and short stories, Sebbar also wrote for the newspaper *Sans Frontière*, which caters for the Third World immigrant population of France, and which also features in this work.

Sherazade is set in Paris, where the author has lived for the past twenty years, but it is not the conventional Paris known to tourists, and the English reader may have difficulty recognizing the topography where her protagonists act out their marginalized or clandestine existence: the squats and flea markets, the working-class districts of Barbès, Jaurès, Crimée, around the Metro stations and boulevards of those names, where many immigrant families have congregated; the outer suburbs of Vanves and Le Kremlin-Bicêtre to the south and Bobigny to the north-west – with their bleak high-rise housing estates – and the Fleury-Mérogis Prison to the south of the capital . . . However, if tourists are not familiar with the Horloge (Clocktower) area in the Halles – the site of the old food markets – where Julien lives, they will easily recognize the Pompidou Centre for Art and Culture (Beaubourg) and the Forum des Halles with its many fashion boutiques, the haunt of Sherazade, Zouzou and France.

Except for Julien Desrosiers, the cast consists of drop-outs, delinquents, drug-addicts, runaways, revolutionaries, and the porn-merchants and yuppies who attempt to exploit them and usually end by being ripped off in their turn. The former are all children of the immigrant proletariat: from Guadaloupe and Martinique, from Morocco, Tunisia, Algeria, Poland – mechanics, car-assembly workers for Renault or Citroën, dustmen, mineworkers. These youngsters – their ages range from seventeen to twenty-seven – are part of the youthful sub-culture of Paris: independent, unassimilated, unscrupulous, often intelligent, sometimes violent, very much as Julien's film-director friend envisages the heroine of his projected film: '. . . a gang-leader, rebel, poet, unruly, adept with a knife, expert at karate, fearless, a fugitive from ZUPs, hanging around housing estates, basements, underground carparks, wandering the streets, as illusive and frightening as a war-leader . . .' It could be London, New York, any large city with an ethnic mix and rootless, alienated youth. But these are, for the most part, Beurs, the untranslatable name given to the second generation North Africans, born or growing up in France, with their own independent radio station, Radio Beurs, and catered for by the newspaper *Sans Frontière*.

There are no gratuitous descriptions, but Leïla Sebbar catches their individual voices, especially in the long unpunctuated passages in Flaubertian *style indirect libre*, the spoken or unspoken 'stream of consciousness' which she transcribes with faultless accuracy and through which her characters reveal the essentials of their backgrounds and experiences.

The eponymous heroine shares many of the characteristics of her streetwise companions and squat-mates; she is wayward, insolent, impulsive, exploitative, fearless and totally amoral. She works peripatetically in fashion boutiques in the Halles district, but supplies her basic needs by shoplifting. She takes part in burglaries and armed hold-ups. Yet she seems to retain a certain intransigent innocence, purity even. She is never tempted by drugs nor the easy opportunities of casual prostitution, like her compatriot Djamila. But what distinguishes her above all is the poetry she writes in secret, showing to no one, and her passion for reading, especially about her native Algeria, which she left as a child and yearns to revisit. Before running away from home she spent all her leisure in the local municipal library, where the friendly librarian ordered shelvesful of books by Algerian writers. It is in the library of the Pompidou Centre at Beaubourg, where she continues her reading, that she attracts the attention of Julien, himself a dedicated Arabist. He introduces Sherazade to more works about Algeria and also Orientalist paintings, of which he is a collector. In the final resort it is the strange attraction of Matisse's *Odalisque in Red Trousers* which decides her to leave Julien and her mates and set out for Algeria.

Many of the characters in this work are obsessive: Krim, with his passion for motorbikes (particularly the powerful Japanese models which his English counterparts affectionately call 'Yammies' and 'Kwakkers'); Pierrot, the hardline militant, with his revolutionary fervour; Sherazade, fascinated by everything Algerian; Julien, with his twin passions for Orientalist paintings and the cinema. It is no gratuitous detail that one of Julien's favourite films is Jean-Luc Godard's illusive, unclassifiable *Pierrot le fou*, made in 1965, from the novel *Obsession* by Lionel White, two years after Godard had actually appeared himself in Gaspard-Huit's film *Shéhérazade*! The fragmented narrative with its sense of immediacy, the early Parisian scenes, the *cinéma vérité* technique, some of the episodes and the frequent references to paintings in Godard's *Pierrot le fou* (Renoir, Velasquez) are mirrored in Sebbar's novel. In the film, a respectable young writer, living a sheltered uneventful life, is fascinated by an enigmatic girl and flees with her from Paris. Godard's Pierrot is paralleled by the two men in love with Sherazade: the writer and scholar Julien, and the revolutionary Pierrot. Godard's Pierrot amuses himself driving his car into the sea, and finally kills himself by tying dynamite round his head, lighting the fuse and blowing his head off; Sebbar's Pierrot takes up Sherazade's challenge to drive the car into the Loire. Unbeknown to her it is loaded with smuggled arms. He crashes it and dies in the explosion. Sherazade is unharmed and disappears before the police arrive on the scene. Sebbar takes up her story in *Les Carnets de Shérazade* (Sherazade's Notebooks, 1985) and *La Fou de Shérazade*, 1990. Neither is as yet translated into English.

Dorothy S. Blair

Sherazade

'Your name's really Sherazade?'

'Yes.'

'Really? It's ... it's so ... How can I put it? You know who Sheherazade was?'

'Yes.'

'And that doesn't mean anything to you?'

'No.'

'You think you can be called Sherazade, just like that? ...'

'No idea.'

He looked at her, standing the other side of the high, round counter at the fast-food, unable to believe his eyes.

'And why not Aziyade?'

'Who's that?'

'A beautiful Turkish woman from Istanbul who Pierre Loti was in love with, a hundred years ago.'

'Pierre Loti I've heard of. Not Aziyade.'

1

'He dressed as a Turk and learned the Turkish language for her sake. He even went to live in the poor district of Istanbul to see her in secret. Aziyade belonged to the harem of an old Turk. She was a young Circassian slave, converted to Islam.'

'Why you telling me about this woman? She's got nothing to do with me.'

'She had green eyes, like you.'

'That's not a reason.'

Sherazade was drinking her Coke out of the can. She wasn't listening any more. Julien Desrosiers went back to reading the small ads in *Libération*.

When Sherazade cupped her hands over the headphones of the walkman hanging round her neck and clamped them over her ears, she broke the red and yellow rayon thread of the scarf with shiny fringes, favoured by Arab women from the Barbès neighbourhood and those fresh from the backwoods who haven't yet been attracted to the scarves sold at Monoprix stores that imitate designer label ones with muted colours and abstract designs. Sherazade didn't much care for this scarf, whose poor-quality material was too soft and slippery so the lead of the walkman got tangled up in it every time the material slipped, as a single knot was never enough to hold it in place; but those mornings when she decided to wear it, the loud colours that betrayed its shoddy quality gave her a sort of perverse pleasure

2

which she made no attempt to show, as if the faint sunlight on the orange formica of the fast-food could make you believe it was summer. Besides, she knew she had to be careful of these almost phosphorescent colours which made her conspicuous and which she couldn't always manage to hide under the collar of her blouson jacket. Anyway the *keffiyeh*, the Palestinian cotton scarf with black and white checks that she'd never been separated from for weeks, would also call police attention to her. She's noticed more than once that youngsters wearing a *keffiyeh*, whose white soon turns grey if it's not washed regularly, are stopped by one of the cops patrolling the Forum or the Metro. Some of them hadn't got identity papers and the cops threatened to turn them in for loitering with intent but didn't do anything. They had to keep on repeating the warning until one day a cop got the idea of unrolling the scarf tied round the youngster's neck and saw a square of white paper slip out that anyone could spot. The kid tried to get his foot on it but the cop was too quick for him and already had it under his heavy black uniform shoe that the kid stared at desperately without moving, as he was held in an iron grip by the two other policemen who were admiring their colleague's accurate flair. The cop had picked up the dose, shaken out the scarf, folded it up, tucked it under his navy-blue arm, to be produced in evidence, and marched the

3

boy off. He was a minor. He was taken to the Quai de Gesvres.* Sherazade had had to replace her *keffiyeh* by the Barbès scarf.

* Quai de Gesvres, Paris headquarters of the police section dealing with juveniles. (Trans.)

Julien Desrosiers

Between two columns of small ads, Julien Desrosiers watched this girl who said her name was Sherazade and who'd so abruptly broken off a conversation that had scarcely begun. He'd promised himself several times he'd speak to her. He often saw her at the library but he'd never managed to find out what she was reading or get a chance of saying anything to her. She always came alone. She'd sit down without a glance at anyone, read and go away again. Once he'd decided to follow her but when she caught sight of him she'd given him such an insolent look that he'd never done it again. That was when he'd seen her green eyes. Even when he managed to get a seat facing her, she always kept her eyes on the book she happened to be reading, and till then he'd never been able to catch her looking at him.

5

Finally he'd wondered if she knew he was sitting at the same table, in the same reading room, sometimes quite near her, so near that he could have touched her by stretching out his arm, or bumped her shoulder as he passed between the tables to get to the shelves.

He came nearly every day. He lived quite near; he'd got a newly built flat in the Horloge district, through the Paris Municipality, light and clean where he could work at his drawing-table, when he didn't have to give his computer lectures and didn't spend the morning or the afternoon at the Louvre, the Salle Drouot, the Bibliothèque Nationale or the School of Oriental Languages. On Sunday mornings he went very early to the flea markets in Montreuil, Vanves, Kremlin-Bicêtre. He worked late into the night. He liked that. Sometimes he went to parties at two or three in the morning, but recently he'd been bored with them. He'd go back there with Sherazade. That's what he told himself when he saw her standing in the fast-food. She'd watched him come in as if she'd always known him. Since she smiled at him, he made his way to her table. If she hadn't smiled he'd have gone to sit at a table in the corner where he could see the whole room and people coming and going. Did she know he was the man from the library, or had she smiled at random and he'd thought she was smiling at him? She'd watched him as he moved over towards her eyes. But here, without the violence of her anger, they seemed almost too gentle.

He said, 'My name's Julien.'

And she, 'Mine's Sherazade.'

Delacroix

She was about to leave.

The metal headband of the walkman had flattened the tight curls on top of her head. She tied another knot in her scarf and it was only then that Julien thought of the picture he liked to linger in front of, all by himself, as no one ever stopped to look at these women who couldn't have been mentioned in the foreign guides or guides for the use of foreigners, among the works of art that you had to have seen if you visited Paris or the Louvre. No one in front of the *Reclining Odalisque* either, or *The Turkish Bath*. But he preferred *The Women of Algiers*. That scarf with its debased Oriental appearance, too yellow and too red, and just to look at it you could sense the poor-quality synthetic fibre, because this girl tied it in front of him, like the Arab women in the little village of Oranie, in the courtyard and the schoolhouse where his father taught, in the *mechtas* where his mother took him when she went to nurse the women and children, Sherazade's hands, her fingers that pulled the ends of the scarf into a knot that would not come undone straight away and then as an afterthought making a double knot, these gestures moved Julien so much that he had to hold on to the edge of the table. Sherazade noticed nothing of all that. She only learned later who these Algerian women were that Julien had thought about because of the cheap scarf she'd put on that day. When she went to the Louvre with him to see *The Women of Algiers*, she noticed that the woman on the left leaning on one elbow, with her legs folded under her on a red and gold *fouta*, had green eyes.

'It's true. It's incredible! Yes, you're right. She's got green eyes.'

He'd stared at Sherazade, putting his hands on her shoulders.

'Just like you.'

Several times they'd both hurried in to see the Delacroix, then out again without seeing anything except these women because that was what they came for, just for them. When they walked along the embankments, Julien talked of the pink in the hair of the woman with the hookah, the *kanoun* on the floor between the three women, the gold bracelets on their naked ankles, the beautiful Negress's hand, the black and red *fouta* with the narrow stripes round her

9

hips below a short midnight-blue bolero, the way the standing Negress looked at her indolent white mistresses. He told Sherazade about the women of the harems, Delacroix's and Fromentin's North Africa, the Arab farmworkers and the poor-white settlers he'd known in Algeria, the street children he'd always played with.

'And the war?' asked Sherazade.

'That's another story.'

Julien had no desire to talk about the Algerian War, after the Louvre.

Nedroma

Julien's father had left a little town in the Department of Charente to come to teach in Algeria.
First of all in a tiny village, then in Nedroma. He
had met other teachers, Frenchmen for the most
part, and some Arabs, 'Natives' educated at the
Bouzarea Teachers' Training College in Algiers.
That's how he'd heard of Mouloud Feraoun, a
poor peasant's son like so many who had been
encouraged by their village teacher to get to this
Training College in Algiers, a mirage and a
miracle. Julien had often listened to his father's
friends talking, teachers in the Oran and Tlemcen regions, in Hennaya, Nemours. Aïn-
Temouchent . . . when they met in a dim classroom to set up a network to provide help in the
form of cash or medical supplies for the Moujahideen. His father didn't stop him coming into
this classroom and Julien understood, without it
being spelled out, that he was supposed to stand

guard. Afterwards, his father and friends went over to the schoolhouse for coffee or tea and the cakes his mother had baked for them; she was just as good at Arab cooking as French cooking. The daughter of French settlers, she had left her home near Setif in Eastern Algeria and moved to the Oran area when she fell in love. She would have liked to become a doctor, but settlers' families were not very keen on girls getting an education at that time. Like all colonial girls at the village school, she had learned to sew, embroider, look after a house and a farmyard and the garden adjoining the farmhouse. Her father had insisted on teaching the girls as well as the boys to shoot. They rode over the vast plateaux given over to cereal crops and the girls galloped headlong just like their brothers. They could fire a pistol or a rifle as well as their mothers and grandmothers who, at the turn of the century, never left the house without a tiny pistol in the deep pocket of their peasant skirts, when they went to keep an eye on the sowing with two or three Arab farmhands, three miles from the village. These women got up at three in the morning, harnessed the horse and drove the cart to the fields. The men were off fighting. Julien's mother had been brought up by these strong, hardy pioneers who could embroider, manage a farm property, fire a rifle, gallop over the high plateaux, nurse and deliver the women in the *mechtas*, go the rounds with their boxes of medecines, give injections, help the teachers in the sewing-classes. Later, when they had left Algeria for good, after the war, Julien's mother showed him one day the detailed reports on the 'Training Courses for Native Girls' in a town school and a country school respectively:

RUE MARENGO PRIMARY SCHOOL, ALGIERS
  Headmistress: Mlle Quetteville

- five classes;
- 170 pupils in the school;
- sixteen full-time apprentices, joined in the afternoon by the pupils from the two top classes;
- fourteen tall-warp looms;
- several small looms and frames for embroidery and lace-making. When the girls become expert, they are paid, with double rate for work done over and above the fixed daily task. Bonuses are added for particularly well-executed work. This school produces carpets, copied from antique Persian and Copt designs, also cushions, Turkish, Algerian and Moroccan embroidery and needle-lace.

BUDGET: income from sale of work and a subsidy of 2000 francs from the Government.

SCHOOL CANTEEN: two pupils from each of

13

the three top classes take turns to cook the midday meal and see to the cleanliness of the canteen.

- Apprentices and pupils are taught domestic work:
● Monday, overalls, towels, loom-covers are washed, heavy laundry done twice a month;
● Tuesday, mending, darning stockings;
● Wednesday, ironing, with and without starch;
● Friday, scouring out saucepans, copper-ware;
● Saturday, general clean-out of kitchen, refectory and workroom.

PREPARATION OF TROUSSEAU: This work undertaken by Mlle Quetteville is very interesting. The basic materials are supplied by sympathizers who have formed a committee. The work is done by the pupils who make a trousseau on Thursday afternoons which will be given them when they reach the age of sixteen.

This trousseau comprises:
- a town outfit complete with *haïk* and velvet embroidered bodice;
- two indoor costumes, one for winter, one for summer.
- two veils adorned with embroidery and lace;
- four chemises;

14

- six handkerchiefs;
- six hand towels;
- six dusters;
- three pairs of stockings;
- one silk scarf.

SCHOOL AT AÏT-HICHEM (near Michelet)

This was one of the first schools open to children of both sexes (1890). The workshop was awarded a prize at the International Exhibition of 1900 for its dressmaking and embroidery work.

In 1913 the school comprises:
- thirty-four pupils aged thirteen to sixteen;
- eight looms.

The pupils are not paid a fixed wage but receive small sums to encourage them.

SCHOOL BUDGET:
- Subsidy from Government;
- Subsidy from the mixed Commune;
- Income from the sale of work to the Natives and tourists.

At first, the pupils were taught by their teacher how to make so-called deep-pile carpets, but wool was expensive in the area. To save money, another teacher introduced them to the method of doing the genuine Berber low-pile weaving which makes a hard-wearing fabric with very original geometric patterns, using the technique rediscovered by M. Ricard. This weaving has become the speciality of Aït-Hichem, but the girls are still taught to make deep-pile carpets. The school subsists on the sympathy of the local inhabitants. The notables let their daughters attend as long as possible and former pupils send their sisters and daughters.

Julien read to the end of these pages and promised himself he would do some research into primary schoolteachers in Algeria, at the Overseas Archives in Aix-en-Provence, but he got bitten by a passion for Orientalist painting and gradually discovered he had all the sublime faults of a collector.

The War of Independence did not put a stop to Julien's mother's nursing activities. She went off fearlessly, just as her grandmother had done, and she even gave first aid to a wounded man, the husband of an Arab woman whom she'd just delivered, with the help of the old village midwife-healer, certainly a Moujahid, but she hadn't asked any questions. She'd mentioned it to her husband when she got home and he hadn't warned her against this. He knew she'd go just the same, but she didn't take Julien with her any more, as she did when he was small, before the war.

Bouzarea

The Native teachers, Arabs and Berbers, his father's friends, spoke French. Julien's mother knew Arabic, Julien could speak and understand a bit, but his father had never managed to learn it. Those evenings Julien did not go off to bed. He stayed up in the sitting-room with the adults who chatted and listened to the radio for the news. These men had been children. Julien was surprised every time they spoke of them, little boys. Some of them were born in Tenes, some in Cherchell, others in Marnia or M'Sila. One of them had told of his childhood in Tenes between 1920 and 1925. His mother had been widowed with five children. He was the oldest. At five in the morning he went to the Qur'anic School until half-past seven. He had a cup of coffee and a little bit of dry bread. From eight till eleven, then from one till four in the afternoon it was the French school. At half-past four till nightfall it was back to the Qur'anic School. The evening meal was very light, the teacher from Tenes emphasized. He went to bed at nine o'clock after doing his homework by the light of a candle or paraffin lamp. On Thursdays he worked as a porter at the market to earn a little money. Sunday mornings also. On Thursday afternoons he did odd jobs for his mother, fetching water for the laundry and to wash with. On Sunday afternoons, he went back to the Qur'anic School. When he was twelve he had to work the whole summer as an auctioneer's messenger, valet, waiter, to earn enough to buy the obligatory outfit for the Boufarik boarding school. He was always top in maths but couldn't understand the *Iliad* or the *Odyssey* at all. He was to enter the Engineering College at Maison-Carrée, near Algiers. He didn't have a certificate of French nationality. So he applied to the teacher-training college to become a Native pupil-teacher. He was accepted the same year as Mouloud Feraoun: 'On 28 September, we were all at Bouzarea with our suitcases and our cheap suits, bought at the Chartres market. The Algiers teacher-training college was France's second largest; for a hundred and eighty French pupil-teachers there were twenty Algerians. Emmanuel Roblès was a second-year student, he ran the college magazine which was called *The Profane*. The young pupil-teachers did their first teaching practice in schools in the Casbah opposite the

18

Barberousse Prison. The boys would make obscene remarks in Arabic to test out the teacher. If he didn't react, he was a Roumi . . . Then they either helped him or played him up . . . The first time I went to France on a school journey, I was overwhelmed by the amount of water: I saw lakes, rivers, ponds everywhere, and by the size of the trees . . . In Paris we did all the sights. When I got back my mother said, "I thought that people who went to France came back fat and well, and you're pale and skinny." On 1 October 1935 I was appointed to El-Bordj, twenty miles from Mascara. I had fifty-six pupils. At the end of the first month I had earned 988.12 francs. With my brother who had accompanied me we ate noodles with eggs, cutlets, cakes and plenty of peanuts . . .

'After El-Bordj, the little school at Aflou on the High Plateaux of Djebel-Amour saw me arrive with my wife, a Frenchwoman from France, on 15 September 1940. The following year I had a son. We rode a lot at that time . . .'

Later, some of the friends of Julien's father were imprisoned by the French, others killed in the maquis. In France, where he'd returned to his family's village in Charente, his father heard that Mouloud Feraoun and other Algerians had been murdered by an OAS commando. Julien saw his father weep when he heard the news on the radio. From Algeria, his mother had only brought back linen, crockery, the family photograph

19

album, some picture postcards and some minor Orientalist pictures that Julien had recently taken out of suitcases stored in his flat. He had covered a whole wall with them. It was strange. The family property on the Setif plateaux had become an agricultural cooperative. The house was occupied by Arab families and surrounded by reed or wooden fences. His mother had gone back there alone, with her sisters, to pay her respects to the family dead. Like many repatriates, she wanted to check the state of the graves, see that they were kept clean and the tombstones in place. The women were very devoted to the dead and went to visit them, to make sure they were still there, and that the graves had not been desecrated as happened to some during the war. Their dead were all right. They were keen to leave them safe, protected by their solid tombstones or their vaults. They had died on the soil where they were born, for all those who had had to expatriate themselves and who would never return to live and die here. Certain women had refused to return to Algeria. They waited to die in exile, in a foreign land, in the cold and mist, complaining softly.

As for certain French people from Algeria, repatriated to France, Algeria after 1962 did not exist, and as they had left nothing living there, only furniture, Henri II-style dining-room suites, pianos . . . pilgrimages were organized to the cemeteries where the women could find their dead again. Julien's mother had been about to spend one or two weeks in Tlemcen for one of these spring pilgrimages, but she had no dead relatives there so she gave up the idea. A Tunisian woman had told her with tears in her eyes of the first return after the exodus. A brother had been buried in the little French cemetery surrounded by cypresses just like in France, the sort of cypresses which nearly always enclosed large farms in North Africa and particularly in Algeria, owned by settlers. She and her sister had searched several times for the grave without being able to find it. They had persisted and went back every day as if their brother's name would suddenly strike the foot or catch the eye of one of the two women, until one day an Arab came up to them and said, 'Are you looking for the grave of . . .? It's over there.' That man had recognized them, twenty years later. He had always looked after the cemetery, he lived close by and had seen them, day after day, loyally, anxiously walking round the graveyard, up and down the paths, leaving to put off to the next day the search which they were unwilling to give up. One morning he had waited for them and slowly approached them. He told them correctly the name of the deceased and showed them where the grave was. He told them the truth. They wondered why they hadn't looked in that corner. That stone on which they could read the name, the dates of his birth and death, and a few words of a conventional epitaph nearly effaced.

As they left the cemetery with tears in their eyes, they thanked the Tunisian who shook their hands warmly.

Pierrot

Sherazade left the fast-food without a glance at Julien. He nearly got up and followed her. To run and catch up with her, talk to her some more. He did nothing. He just watched her through the glass door.

Before she came to live in one, Sherazade had never heard the word. She didn't even know it was English. It sounded like that strange name they called Red Indian women in the comics her brothers read, and when they played indoors on rainy days, she acted the squaw, according to her brothers' scenario. She hadn't thought to ask if it was English, American or Indian. She would have rather thought it was a word in the Indian language, but she wasn't sure. When her brothers told her, 'We're going to play cowboys and Indians with the cowboys attacking the Indian camp,' she knew she'd be the squaw with

23

her baby tied on her back. She'd been quite happy to play the squaw until the time she'd been kidnapped by the Whitemen on horseback. She'd quarrelled with her brothers as they said the squaw had to stay at home by the tent with the children and the other women and during the attacks she wasn't allowed to go near the river. Sherazade had escaped and gone outside the camp; it was near the river that the Whitemen on horseback had surprised her, leaning over the water; they had snatched her up, slung her on to a horse and carried her off riding pillion behind one of them to the train to the nearest American town.

After this episode her brothers didn't play Cowboys and Indians with her any more; but she still saw the word written and read it though her brothers never pronounced it again.

She remembered that exact word when she heard – *squat* – for the first time. Pierrot had suggested she come to live in the old building where he was squatting with his mates. She'd made him repeat the foreign word, so he'd explained that he lived with some boys and girls in an empty flat that they didn't pay rent for as the building was due to be demolished. He added, 'But where d'you come from? Everybody knows what squatting means? Don't you go out or anything?'

'I'm from Aulnay-sous-Bois, from the Mille-Mille.'

'Then you must know Krim. He comes from there too. But he's from the Trois Mille or thereabouts . . .'

'Aulnay-sous-Bois is a big place.'

'I'm sure your father works at Citroën,' Pierrot added.

'Yes.'

Djamila

Pierrot had given Sherazade the address of the
squat and ever since she'd been living there she
always spoke and thought of it as 'the squat'.
She shared a room with Djamila, a girl who'd
turned up one evening with Krim. He'd met her
in Rue Saint-Séverin where she'd been looking
for the number of a building she'd jotted down
on a torn envelope in Marseilles before leaving.
She was sure of finding someone but she soon
realized the number didn't exist. The street
wasn't that long. She hadn't thought to check it
on a map of Paris. They'd laughed at her in the
first café she'd gone into to ask. She'd drunk a
cup of coffee at the counter to give herself time to
find another address in the spiral notebook
whose cover was half falling off. It was a girls'
hostel. She'd been told she could stay there a few
nights. The café proprietor who she asked to
show her the way grumbled that it wasn't just

26

next door and it was impossible to explain and she'd get lost if she was a stranger thereabouts.

As she insisted, he asked his wife, who was at the cash-desk, for the map of Paris which he opened up on the counter so that Djamila could follow the fat red finger which slowly wandered over the map. He wasn't a Parisian. He came from Aveyron like nearly all the café proprietors in Paris. His brain seized up in front of a map. After a few minutes, when the finger grew stiffer and stiffer and was coming to a halt just any-where, Djamila suggested she look at the map herself on an empty table, at the back of the café, near the toilet-and-telephone area, which stank as usual. She knew how to read a map. She had found her way to Paris on her own, with a road map. She'd left in such a hurry that she hadn't had time to take her mother's cheque-book that she'd intended to use for the train tickets. She had fifty francs in her pocket. She'd crossed France somehow to get to Paris where she had no idea what she was going to do. Why Paris? She knew no one there, whereas in the Bassens housing estate where she'd been living for years, she couldn't walk three yards without having to greet someone in French or Arabic with, 'Hi! How are things?' Among the girls on the estate she'd been the only one to pass her *baccalauréat* in a year when several had tried. She'd decided long ago to leave as soon as she had her certifi-cate. She'd said so to her mother, explaining she

27

absolutely had to go to Algeria to find her father and brothers who she hadn't seen for nearly ten years. Her mother was a Frenchwoman who'd had a job at the check-out in a supermarket in Marseilles when her father married her. In spite of having seven children, her mother had always gone on working. The father, a mechanic in a garage, had gone off one day, leaving his wife to bring up the five girls, taking the two boys with him, the eldest and the youngest of the children. The mother had done everything to try to get her sons back but nothing helped. The father, an Algerian, didn't have to answer for his actions to France, once he'd settled in Algeria with his Algerian sons. Djamila's mother heard nothing more of this man who'd been her husband, nor of her two sons. She hadn't had the courage to go to Algeria to look for her children and everybody who'd tried to help her had dissuaded her. Djamila heard from an Algerian who worked in the garage, where she used to drop in to see her father on her way to school, that he'd gone back to the Setif district where he was born and had set up a garage there. It was doing well because second-hand cars there could be repaired till they were only fit for the scrap-heap. 'Car-repairing is a gold-mine,' the Algerian had said. Djamila's father had married again, a cousin from Setif whose father had a little shop. Everything was fine for him. Djamila had insisted on the Algerian telling her the name of her father's village. The Algerian hesitated, then wrote it for her on the bus ticket she held out to him.

Djamila showed the ticket to her mother who just about managed to read it. She'd never been to Algeria and she wasn't very keen on Arabs either. Djamila had realized this one evening when she'd overheard her parents quarrelling. She hadn't wanted to eavesdrop but she couldn't help hearing her mother's voice as her Marseilles accent got even more marked when she shouted and she couldn't forget the words she kept repeating through her sobs, 'Go back to your own country,' and her father, who rolled his Rs, shouting back, 'I'm going tomorrow.' One morning he wasn't to be seen, and the boys didn't return to their respective schools where their father had gone to meet them to catch the plane.

Djamila's mother didn't try to understand why her daughter wanted to go to Algeria. She pointed to the door and said she could leave, she wouldn't stop her.

Instead of taking the boat to Algiers, Djamila had turned up in Paris, not really knowing how. She hadn't forgotten her passport nor the paper showing she'd passed her first qualifying exam.

In Rue Saint-Séverin, Krim suggested the squat. She followed him. Sherazade had been there for a few weeks already. She offered Djamila the other mattress as every room was occupied. Driss told Krim he wasn't to bring a new boy or girl every day, there were enough of them already as it was, the flat wasn't a dormitory or a home for down-and-outs and he'd kick the next ones out himself. Krim swore at him in Arabic and Driss who hadn't got up when Djamila arrived, jumped to his feet ready to start a fight. Krim regularly attended the classes in unarmed combat at a gym where fellows of his age, often Arabs, Algerians and Moroccans, trained like crazy. Quick, agile and aggressive, they had the qualities that the instructors looked for and if they hadn't registered in such large numbers as soon as the lists opened the trainers would have gone into the housing estates to recruit them. But they came of their own accord, two or three at a time, or in gangs, and they could be seen walking together wearing tracksuits, practising in the Metro, on the platforms, in the trains, lunging out at an imaginary enemy, with the technical shouts that they learned in the classes. The French people from the suburbs stared at them, tired, speechless, anxious. They were scared of getting the corner of an Adidas bag hurled at full speed clipping them on the cheek or the ear. But the boys were so skilful they skimmed but never touched anyone; they provoked, knowing full well that the people sitting around were waiting for the slightest bungled shot to start yelling. They appeared not to see anyone, but they had already spotted the passengers' surly expressions, tight lips, clenched fists. They kept their activity to one square yard, shouting and laughing, using words they were the only ones to understand. Driss knew Krim's strength and skill. He didn't persist but he went on muttering to himself, curled up in the red armchair, in front of the TV.

Krim went into the kitchen with Djamila. Pierrot and Basile were preparing a Caribbean dish and Pierrot was insisting he knew the special spices better than Basile and the right amount for the sauce to go with the fish.

Meriem

Sherazade was in the Metro, on the Etoile-Nation line. She was listening to a little girl who was spelling out the names of all the stations, until every time the train crossed the Seine, she started pulling her mother's face towards the window shouting, 'The Seine, the Seine'. Because of the excitement of the child who was leaving the suburban tenement blocks or subtopian housing development for the first time, she had removed the headphones of the walkman for a moment. Sherazade had decided that day to tune in to the independent radio stations and she had replaced her cassette player with her transistor. As soon as the Metro went underground, Sherazade tuned in to Carbon 14 and stayed with it briefly, whereas the indicator normally moved ceaselessly from one station to another, as she always thought the next one would be better. So the needle moved from left

32

to right, then from right to left, without a break, across the dial on which the marks she'd made to hold the station she liked slipped because of her haste.

She knew the names, the frequencies, the places on the dial of all the stations, and the list of the ones she listened to most often was always on her lips. She could have recited them in order:

Radio-Beurs, Paris 106.1 MHz.

Generation 2 000, Paris 88.4 MHz.

Radio-Tipsy, Paris 88.8 MHz.

Radio-Libertarian, Paris 84.5 MHz.

NRG (energy), Paris 92 MHz.

Rock Boulevard, Paris 94.6 MHz.

Radio-Tomato, Paris 94.2 MHz.

Carbon 14, Paris 97.30 MHz.

Radio Sunshine, Paris 98.2 MHz.

Judaic, Paris 103.35 MHz.

Carbon 14 was broadcasting messages like many other stations, but this time Sherazade stopped looking round her to concentrate on listening to the radio. She'd just heard her own first name. She knew it was uncommon and didn't immediately grasp that it really was her name; someone was sending her a message. The person who was reading the message had paused after 'Sherazade' to say, 'I'd really like to meet the girl who's got that name, if it isn't a false name . . . Because when you're called "Sherazade" . . .' He repeated the name several times, then broke off to give this Sherazade the telephone number of the station, if she wanted to ring she'd be given a free hand, she could do and say anything, everything . . . with a name like that . . . Sherazade was growing impatient. Was he never going to read that message. With the independent radio stations it was always like that, endless wisecracks . . . this time, it was serious. She pressed the headphones tight to her ears. The announcer was still wise-cracking. At the next public phone, when she got out of the Metro, she'd let him have a mouthful. That would stop his jaw for him. She'd forgotten she was in the compartment, she was going to shout to the fellow to shut up. She heard, 'Sherazade, it's me, Meriem. Just say you're alive.' Sherazade snatched off the headphones, rushed out on to the platform, tore up the escalators, jostling the protesting users, ran along the boulevard to a phone box.

She knew the number by heart. The money was ready in the left pocket of her jacket. She hung up before hearing the phone ring in her own home.

Sherazade

The day Julien Desrosiers had first spoken to
Sherazade, because of this name that he'd heard
pronounced *Sheherazade*, with an aspirated H
and rolled R, by an Arab who'd called out to her
in the square in front of Beaubourg, a pal from
the squat, Driss, who Julien would never get to
know, as during all the weeks that he was to put
her up, she never mentioned him once, in spite
of his frequent allusions to the evenings and the
nights when she didn't come back to his place,
that day Sherazade happened not to have put on
her Mexican boots or her red shoes with pointed
toes and stiletto heels that she liked to wear with
black fishnet stockings to visit nightclubs, pre-
tending to be a bimbo according to Pierrot, who
couldn't stand black stockings especially fishnet,
he thought they made her look like a tart and
Sherazade retorted, 'You would, wouldn't you, a
square old militant like you.'

'Not so old as all that. I'm twenty-seven. You're not going to tell me I look like Krivin. Besides, I haven't got a tie.'

'Krivin, who's he? Never heard of him.'

'You're just an ignoramus.'

That day, Sherazade was wearing white tennis shoes, useful if she had to make a dash for it after shoplifting in the superstores, which was often less risky than in small boutiques. Besides, she'd tried on these tennis shoes in the sports department of a big store, Porte d'Italie or Montparnasse with its hundred and one boutiques, or it might have been Galaxie, eventually she forgot exactly where she'd nicked things, as quickly as she forgot the things themselves that she deposited at the bottom of a cupboard and that everybody in the squat used. However, she hadn't planned anything that morning as she laced up the soft white leather shoes that she'd left the shop wearing, first walking very fast then breaking into a run, leaving behind an old pair of cheap boots that her mother had gone with her to buy at Monoprix when the sales were on. The leather uppers had cracked the first time she was out in the rain and the soles hadn't lasted long in the mud of the housing estate. She was still wearing them the day she'd decided to leave for good and she took the first opportunity of jettisoning them on the mottled grey carpet at the feet of the disgusted assistant who'd been too slow to react, taking a few hesitating steps behind Sherazade, shouting 'Mademoiselle! Mademoiselle!' as she pushed open the door and ran off towards the Metro. The assistant had let her try on several pairs of tennis shoes, even lending her a pair of white socks with red and blue stripes which were kept for customers, in spite of her surprise at the bare feet emerging from the old boots. She'd been patient with this girl whom she ought to have been suspicious of and who'd wasted her time as she obsessively fingered the leather and compared the leather of the different pairs, finally deciding on the most expensive ones. 'Mademoiselle! Mademoiselle!' The saleswoman nearly sprained her left ankle on her way back to the department. She sat down on the seat Sherazade had just vacated and furiously kicked at the boots left lying on the carpet. The manageress watched her. She couldn't say anything. The assistant wasn't to blame. The next time they'd have to be more suspicious of that sort of girl.

'Take those boots and throw them away.'

The assistant got up, picked up the boots with the fingers of one hand while holding her nose with the other, and threw them in the large wastepaper-basket near the cash-desk.

'Selima, wrap them up. It looks bad,' the manageress said. 'Or else put them in an empty box.'

For the red shoes, Sherazade had been more cautious. She'd hankered after them for a long

37

time, even if eventually she hadn't worn them often. She'd chosen a fairly big shop, crowded with customers and saleswomen. She'd asked to see five different styles including the red ones, she'd tried them all on to make sure the red ones suited her; she'd told the assistant the red ones didn't really fit and while she went down to find the size bigger, Sherazade had put the pair of shoes in her bag under a pullover and shut the box which she placed under the others. She waited patiently, tried on the last pair which were too big. She thanked the assistant nicely who'd had to go back and forth twice to get the boxes down, said goodbye before the empty box disappeared under the other three, and left with a smile. She turned at the corner of the first street and went into a café. In the *Ladies*, she'd nearly made a mistake and gone into the *Gentlemen* at the bottom of the stairs that she'd raced down, she took out the shoes and gazed at them as long as the fluorescent switch that had to be pressed for the light to come on permitted.

That evening, back at the squat, she showed them off to the others. Pierrot thought them ridiculous and it was Djamila who wore them more often than Sherazade.

Pierrot

When Sherazade came out of the phone box she ran all the way till she got back to the room she had to herself until Djamila arrived. The door was ajar. She couldn't see anyone. She rushed to her bed and threw herself face down on the red cover that she had swopped at the flea market for a bundle of polka-dotted blouses, fifties style.

She lay sobbing.

Krim, Basile and Pierrot were practising the electric guitar, banjo and drums, in a room they'd fixed up with salvaged sheets of cork. They also had a zither and an acoustic guitar that the father of one of their pals had brought back one day for his son, one of Krim's mates. The father was a dustman, working for the council, in the well-to-do districts and he seldom came home from work without something he'd found to give his wife or children. It was always a surprise. He was a handyman and repaired the toys, furniture, musical instruments that his wife or children decided to keep. So they all felt rich with these treasures that they'd never have found anywhere else, and though their father told them to write 'seasonal worker' where they had to fill in *father's occupation* at the beginning of every school year, they weren't ashamed of his job. They thought, up to the day when they learned, at school most often, that someone who collects rubbish is called a 'dustman' or more usually a 'garbage man', that their father was a 'seasonal worker' a bit like the scrap merchants they saw round the waste ground near the housing estates. Anyway, when they knew the word 'dustman' they didn't connect it with household rubbish. When they were small, the father took the boys, on the days when there was no school, and let them sit in the large cabin in the front of the big green lorry next to the driver, from where they could just glimpse the street. They couldn't see their father working at the back. They were as happy as if they were in a fire-brigade car, or rather a fire-engine, a real red one with siren, hose, ladder and flashing blue light.

When the dustcart drove into the incineration plant, the children stood up in the cabin to watch the operations. Back home, in the evening, they told their sisters and younger brothers who were not yet old enough to be allowed this outing, all about their day. The girls protested but their father was adamant. He promised them even more surprising surprises.

Krim's pal dropped in at the squat now and then with a musical instrument which he lent or gave them and that Pierrot tried to repair. He'd learned how to work with wood and certain metals, in the workshop back home with his father who was a mineworker in Bruay-en-Artois. His father, the son of Polish immigrants, thought if his son was training to be a chemical engineer, as he wanted to, he ought to be capable of doing anything with his hands. Pierrot used to spend his Sundays shut up in the workshops adjoining the garden of the house in the mining village where he'd grown up. It was a fine wooden workshop that Pierrot's father had built himself and divided into two sections: one for his DIY, and the other for his wife who was a dressmaker. It was a sort of sewing-room with a table for cutting out, a long mirror, a dressmaker's dummy and Singer sewing machine that her parents had given her the day she married the Pole. She was French from Douai and never managed to learn Polish that her husband spoke when they went on Sunday afternoons to visit the Polish in-laws. Pierrot couldn't speak his father's language, in spite of the repeated efforts of Polish cousins who Pierrot's father had asked not to speak French to the child. After a few minutes, especially if they were alone, some distance from the house, near the stream at the bottom of the garden, the children began speaking French among themselves, forgetting the family's recommendations. Pierrot knew a few words of Polish that he forgot in Paris. But whenever the need arose, Pierrot found he hadn't lost his manual skill in spite of his militant, political activities. Besides, the comrades in his group didn't take long to find out that Pierrot's abilities were valuable to them. It wasn't a matter of repairing a zither or a mandoline. They asked him to teach them, among other things, how to make a Molotov cocktail and also small bombs that you had to know exactly how much explosive to use. Pierrot secretly ran practical courses for his comrades in a sort of cubicle that they'd hurriedly erected at the end of a shed where a scrap merchant stored his material, ignorant of what was going on behind the wooden partitions. He knew the lads, their families, and shared their political ideas – they were all Reds in the working-class districts on the outskirts of the city – the fathers were no longer very militant but the sons were very active without ever talking about what they did. For them, so their sons thought, it was enough to be a Communist.

Basile

One evening, a comrade turned up at the cubicle with a book under his arm and a new recruit. It was Basile. He introduced him as a militant revolutionary from the West Indies. From Guadaloupe, Basile corrected him. He spoke of the armed struggle. They listened to him. He spoke for three hours and was accepted, until the day when he tried to make his comrades listen to the history of the Rasta movement. The militarist militants made fun of this speech and this 'under-developed' tendency. Pierrot was the only one Basile could talk to. Soon they met again at the squat where they were to live together for several months, sharing their passion for music, politics and their fascination with an underground armed revolution which they still believed in, egging each other on to read everything that had been written or told about the Baader-Meinhof Gang, the Red

43

Brigade, the Russian Terrorists, the Palestinian Revolutionaries, the Angolans . . .

They both had managed to get hold of a .38 and some evenings, when they were alone with Sherazade, they played at 'Indians', the name given to the Italian Autonomes.* They took up the position of the .38 marksman, holding the revolver at arm's length, legs apart and knees slightly bent, they closed one eye to take aim, facing each other; at that moment Sherazade instinctively closed her eyes until Basile and Pierrot burst out laughing simultaneously. Sherazade got up and asked Pierrot, 'Will you lend it to me?'

'It's not a toy. It's not for birds . . .'

Sherazade called him macho and asked Basile for his .38.

'Mind out, it's loaded! Here, you hold it like this.'

Basile launched into a long speech explaining that German and Italian women belonged to terrorist groups and could handle weapons as well as the men, they were good for other things besides being used as letter-boxes, couriers, and this was the beginning of equality and if in a revolution women could work as secretaries and nurses they could also be given power, responsibility . . . If Sherazade liked, she could very well

* *Autonomes*, an extreme left-wing group in the 1970s. See also note on p.69. (Trans.)

become head of a network . . . Sherazade interrupted Basile.

'You managing my life for me, now?'

'Me?' Basile shouted. 'Are you a moron? I'm
just saying exactly the opposite!'

'Oh! All right. I didn't understand.'

Pierrot, who hadn't said a word, quoted the
Algerian and Vietnamese women fighters, other
women who had taken part in wars of liberation
and who, when independence was won, found
themselves deprived of the liberty and equality
they'd fought for . . . Sherazade whistled in
admiration.

'You do know a lot . . . if you're in power one
day, it'll be super for women. I'll fight for that.'

She was playing with Basile's .38. The shot
went off smack into the left eye of Che Guevara
whose poster had been yellowing for months on
the wall. Basile yelled out and snatched the .38
out of Sherazade's hands.

'Wait, I was going to have a go at the other . . .'

'What other?'

'That one, next to Marx . . . I know his face.
You see him everywhere.'

'What? Bob Marley!'

'You're crazy, completely crazy!'

'What the hell! They're all dead . . .'

Pierrot and Basile exchanged glances, taken
aback. Sherazade always disconcerted them.

Sherazade turned to Pierrot. 'And now, don't
ever call me a bird again or I'll do you in . . .'

Pierrot moved over to her and put his arms round her. He was going to kiss her neck when he felt something cold against his forehead. It was Basile's .38.

'Not that one, Bill . . .' Sherazade broke loose and they began to laugh.

Krim

They'd been playing one at a time, or in unison, and when they stopped Krim was the first to hear Sherazade crying. They'd work with a tape-recorder, after listening to a piece on the hi-fi that they'd re-purchased cheap from receivers Krim knew well because he did jobs for them on occasion. The tape-recorder was first-rate too. They'd got really good equipment to work with, as Pierrot, who knew what was what, never tired of telling them.

'What are we going to do?'

Up till now, Sherazade had never cried, or at least none of them had ever seen or heard her crying.

'What are we going to do?'

They knew nothing about her. Her first name. And they weren't even sure of that. One day, she'd said her name was Camille Z. Pierrot had asked her to produce her identity papers. She'd flown into a rage.

'You a cop? That's news!'

They'd never mentioned the matter again.

And now she was crying.

None of them said a word. All three were thinking perhaps Sherazade had been crying for ages and they'd been so engrossed in enjoying their music they knew nothing about it. They'd been singing and laughing and drinking lots of beer. They were having a good time and she . . .

Pierrot especially felt upset. More than Krim and Basile, he thought; and immediately – shit. I'm in love. He didn't want to be the first to go into her room. It was impossible. He urged Krim to go and see Sherazade. He knew Krim had a French girlfriend who didn't come to the squat and who he visited at her place. She had a bed-sitter and a job. She was five years older than him. Pierrot didn't know her. He was sure Krim was not in love with Sherazade.

'You go Krim. She quite likes you.'

At that moment the front door slammed and Eddy came in, holding up Driss.

'I found him downstairs, on the pavement. He's drunk I think. He can't get a word out.'

Pierrot helped Driss on to his bed. They were used to finding Driss in this state. He always managed somehow to get back somewhere near the squat, before collapsing in a sort of drunken stupor, when he wasn't in need of a fix. Driss, contrary to other addicts, didn't seek the company of other druggies to chat, shoot up, drink, get stoned together ... He wandered around aimlessly, all by himself and couldn't stand the other junkies. He only met them when he spent the evening at the Kiss Club, staying right through to the small hours. The others dressed the same as him, had the same gestures, the same position as him. He didn't know them and that was all right with him. He wouldn't see them again till he spent the next evening there. No one said much – the music prevented anything being heard – they accepted each other, while preserving their anonymity, just as they were, for the moment, for one night, sitting side by side on the stained imitation leather benches, with holes in them, too narrow to rest on properly.

The squat-mates didn't inject. Some of them smoked pot that they got in Holland or Morocco. Basile also got some from the Caribbean Rastas who pretended they were Jamaicans living in exile in Paris. They had plenty and were sufficiently expert for it always to be good quality. Crack was beginning to get too dear. When they couldn't get it for a reasonable price, or by some fiddle, they did without. They had shown Sherazade how to smoke and to distinguish the adulterated grass that she also used. She didn't smoke much. She said, laughing at herself, she'd rather read. 'It's my drug, my vice.' She smoked with them on the evenings when they threw a party and invited their buddies – to let their hair down.

Driss

They dreaded the state Driss got into when he was strung out. He became violent. They could see him suffering and didn't know what to do. None of them had any smack. Some of Driss's mates who sometimes dropped in were pushers, dealers, but they weren't always around when needed, and they tried to calm Driss who wouldn't listen to anyone and began an endless unbroken monologue:

'He's the one who chucked me out he's a bastard he never loved me he loves the other kids the kids by his second or third wife he doesn't love me I'm the son of the woman he repudiated he sent her back to Morocco back to her village back to her mother with the two youngest and me why did he keep me with him I wanted to go back there where my mother is and he said no he always says no when I want something his latest wife is young he does

50

everything for her and her kids for me nothing he never helped me at school I worked all by myself if I had bad marks he hit me one day he put salt on my wet skin and beat me with his belt when I tell anyone that they don't believe me I've got Arab pals their fathers aren't like that they don't hit them they ask if everything's all right my father the first job I got as a welder with my CAP. he took all my dough and every month he said I had to give him my wages cos he'd spent a lot of money bringing me up in the end I'd had a bellyful I left his wife was only too pleased she always says he's too soft with me I left I wanted to go to Morocco but I hadn't got any dough I wanted to see my mother she's been gone seven years I haven't seen her again my father stops me going back to Morocco I was born there I was five when I came here with my mother first to Gennevilliers and afterwards to Sarcelles when my mother arrived my father was shacked up with a Frenchwoman my mother wanted to go back my father told her he'd leave the Frenchwoman if she'd stay she stayed but it didn't work out my father lived with my mother and he went on seeing the Frenchwoman I saw him once with her in a café I told my mother she knew she quarrelled with my father he repudiated her she left after that my father married a young Moroccan woman a cousin from his village she came here for him when I left my father's place I worked and with the money I went to Morocco to see my mother she'd asked for a divorce I didn't know this she'd remarried a man older than my father but he hadn't any children he was nice to her and took care of my brothers and sisters he works my mother says she's all right but I couldn't stay there with no work and no money my mother's new husband said I could stay but I said no and I think my mother would rather I worked in France I left my mother said I could go there any time I liked but I'm not going back there my father when I came back to his place instead of welcoming me like a father welcomes his son where we come from he locked me in a room and beat me saying he'd been told I was stealing cars I was a hooligan I swore it wasn't true he didn't believe me he said his house wasn't my home any more he cursed me he said he didn't want to see me again I put my things in a case and left I found my old job and lived all alone in an empty house I was miserable I did my own washing and cooked for myself I hadn't got my mother or my sisters or anyone to do all that for me I couldn't stay there but I got to know a girl a French girl who went to college she was head over heels in love with me I quite liked her nothing more I never saw her family nor her house I used to go back with her as far as the corner that's all when I phoned I said it's Philippe and as people say I haven't got an accent they don't take me for an Arab her mother thought I was French she called her

daughter to the phone and so I could talk to her
she told me if her father knew he'd smash my
face in he's her stepfather and he's a cop since
I've been staying here I don't see her any more I
get news of her from a pal he gives me letters
from her but I'm not so keen to see her she's too
keen it's a bloody drag once before I came to live
here a cousin saw me in the street he'd come to
invite me to his wedding I went to the party and
saw my father with his wife and kids I wanted to
say hello he refused to greet me in front of
everybody it was a public insult he disowned
me afterwards I heard he'd been told I was a
junkie and the cops were after me and they'd
been to my father's place and talked about
burglaries and break-ins and my father had
disowned me in front of them and told them if
he saw me if I came back he'd hand me over to
the cops himself I can't afford the smack out of
my pay it's eight hundred francs a gram I'm not
going to sell my arse either so I do some break-
ins and sell what I find so I get money for smack
but with my father it's finished I don't see him
any more he doesn't exist any more I'd rather go
to prison than go back to him . . . '

Driss spat with contempt as he spoke, he
shouted and sobbed and finally fell asleep.

Farid

Pierrot left Eddy keeping an eye on Driss. They had got to know each other in Sarcelles. Eddy dropped in at the squat from time to time to play music with them; he played the sax. When Djamila started to share Sherazade's room, Eddy came more frequently and Driss offered to let him stay in his room.

Basile and Krim were watching TV. Pierrot asked, 'Where's Sherazade?' Krim replied that she was asleep. Pierrot went to her room and peeped through the door that was ajar and looked at her as she slept. The walkman had been thrown on the bed. She was fully dressed. She'd still got on her trainers, her leather jacket; the scarf had slipped to one side, yellow and red on the red bedcover. Pierrot daren't touch her. She wouldn't sleep comfortably in those tight jeans, with her jacket fastened up to her neck and those trainers that must be making her feet perspire. Pierrot didn't like sleeping in his clothes. He always slept naked, even in winter. He approached Sherazade, stretched out a hand towards her, but as she stirred he withdrew it immediately. He continued to watch her. Now and again he heard her give a stifled sob. Near the bed he saw a writing pad and a little black and red notebook. He took a blank sheet of paper and wrote, 'Sherazade, I love you. Pierrot,' and placed the paper near her cheek. She would see it as soon as she woke.

Pierrot went back to join Krim and Basile; after a quarter of an hour he suddenly jumped up out of the red armchair and rushed to Sherazade's room. He heard a sound and stopped. He wanted to tear up the note he'd just written her but he'd put it so close to her cheek that he risked waking her. He looked through the half-open door. She had stirred and crumpled the sheet of paper in her sleep. She turned over and the note disappeared under her short curls. Pierrot moved away and came back to sit in the red armchair. It was a miserable evening. He picked up a plan of the outskirts of Paris and unfolded it on the floor.

The TV was switched on but no one was watching it. Basile was glancing through *Libération* and reading the small ads aloud, Miscellaneous and Lonely Hearts. He was looking for a job. Like Pierrot he'd passed his *baccalauréat*. He'd started studying law at Assas, but regularly got into fights with the Fascists and there were punch-ups nearly every day. He nearly got picked up by the cops. Since then he'd done temps, he'd been a courier, furniture-remover, done washing-up for West-Indians who made him work like a slave. He'd decided to go back to university while doing a period of training with the newspaper *Libération*, but at the end of the training he hadn't found anything. He was still a militant member of a group when he met Pierrot. They'd decided to go off together next holidays if they could get a job as long-distance lorry-drivers in the countries of the Middle East as far as Pakistan. If they liked the work they'd keep on for a year or two. Basile was looking for offers among the small ads. Meanwhile they had to get their heavy-duty driving licences. Naturally they would be travelling through Italy. Pierrot knew that members of the Red Brigade were hiding under assumed names in other Italian groups. They were teaching urban guerrilla tactics to the French and found them good pupils, attentive and conscientious; they were all very young, younger than Pierrot, hardly any of them were more than twenty. It was in one of these groups that Pierrot had met Farid. He was a very idealistic Algerian immigrant, who must have read enthusiastically everything about the Algerian war that he had neither lived through nor

56

known. This history, the history of his own country, had passed him by, like so many others, as he was too young, and because he was an immigrant, living so long in France that it had needed the independence movement to awaken in him a stifled repressed nationalism. He had discovered the exaltation, the determination of those who prepared the war of Algerian liberation, but the cause was no longer the same. It was not so clear-cut, nor so simple. He was a rebel, he would have liked to be a revolutionary. A rebel like Basile, Pierrot, Krim, Driss, all those at the squat and in certain political groups. Pierrot read in *Sans Frontière* of Farid's suicide. Why had he gone to Finland to die? Had he really committed suicide? Basile went to the funeral in a Parisian cemetery with the family, friends and comrades. There was no area reserved for Muslims in the cemetery, and anyway, was Farid a Muslim? He said he was first and foremost an Algerian. In these groups there was no question of religion. They never spoke of it. For the first time Pierrot saw Basile unhappy. He didn't speak a word the whole day. In the evening he asked Eddy to play his sax.

Eddy played the sax for Basile, sitting in the red armchair.

Basile

Krim was eating a sandwich he'd just made for himself; the others were not hungry. He had put too much *harissa* in and was puffing like the deuce, as if to blow out the hot spice . . . He was shaking his hands, snapping his fingers and hopping from one foot to the other, as if to say how much the *harissa* was burning his mouth, tongue and throat. 'Water! water! water!' He ran to the kitchen and drank in silence, in the face of Basile's and Pierrot's show of unconcern.

Pierrot was now examining the plan of Paris. He had left the North when he was about nineteen; though he'd soon have been in Paris for eight years he didn't like this city and didn't know it well. He couldn't understand foreigners' enthusiasm for the capital. For his part, he always followed the same route without paying any attention to Paris. He knew exactly where he'd find his mates for a demo, a meeting or a break-in . . . and since he'd been living at the squat he didn't have to move from one dreary room to another, having to rely on the chance of someone or other putting him up. He lived like an underground revolutionary, never giving his name or address. Basile didn't take himself so seriously, nor was he so serious; more curious, more able to brazen it out when, as he told Pierrot, he gate-crashed fabulous parties where he was actually out of his element, and he was never invited but he nearly always got to know about them from his mates who gave him the tip-off and he turned up just as if he'd been expected. He always managed to dress just right, without overdoing it; he always hit on the correct detail which would draw attention to the originality of his outfit, of which all the other elements, trousers, jacket, shoes were exactly right for this particular party, this particular group where nobody knew him and everyone hung around him because they found him good-looking, self-assured and attractive. So he had built up for himself an evening social life in which the most diverse and antagonistic elements of society found themselves in contact and who, on those occasions, made advances to each other. There, punks, yobbos, businessmen, intellectuals, artists, people in advertising and entertainment all rubbed shoulders. Basile gave faithful accounts of these parties which Pierrot despised, but when Basile talked about them

Pierrot listened and laughed at his imitations, and the way he described and commented on them. In the end he began to admire him for being able to get about so easily, without any hang-ups. He envied this physical and mental freedom which he himself did not have.

Basile didn't tell Pierrot, because he thought he would disapprove, not out of prudery but on political and moral principles, that women chatted him up, sometimes several in one evening; about two or three o'clock in the morning he had to make up his mind which one he would go off with for a hectic end to the night, to be followed by a copious late breakfast in a fine flat with a glassed-in balcony or a conservatory opening off the french-windows. When he ended up in a four-star hotel, he wasn't so pleased. Once he could frankly have kicked himself for landing up there, but it only happened once; if it had happened again he would have given up going to hotels; about eleven o'clock in the morning a Caribbean girl arrived with the breakfast tray, wearing the obligatory white apron and white cap on her straightened hair; she was absolutely businesslike, black skirt, white blouse buttoned up to the neck. He was the person who opened the door. The woman was in the bath. He looked at the chambermaid who looked him straight in the eye; luckily, he had thought to throw a towel round his waist. He took the tray, put it on the table at the end of the bed, dressed quietly, scribbled an unsigned note with a felt pen on a paper napkin, 'Sorry. Urgent appointment.' To the women who picked him up like this he said his name was Louis or Bob, invariably eliciting, 'Like Armstrong . . . or Marley . . .'

'Yes. That's right.'

He left. The woman was singing in the bath. He heard her calling 'Bob! Bob!' He shut the door quietly and recited a prayer that he wouldn't meet the young Caribbean chambermaid, for it was at times like these that the words came back to him that he'd learned in his childhood in churches or from pious grandmothers he'd known in Guadaloupe.

Basile didn't think Pierrot would have called him a gigolo if he'd told him his adventures on the party nights. The women didn't give him any money. He went with the ones he liked and who liked him. That didn't stop him coming back to the squat, continuing his militant activities, making music with his pals. The idea had never crossed his mind that he could make anything out of these encounters and if he happened to see one of the women again, it was because he liked her more than the others. The affair lasted until Basile got the feeling that he was being trapped by himself and by her. He always said he didn't want to fall in love.

Basile stopped reading the small ads and remarked, 'Suppose we went to Africa, Pierrot?'

'To do what?'

'As lorry-drivers. We could go as far as South Africa, Mozambique, Madagascar and all the little islands round about. Pass me your map.'

'It's Paris.'

'What are you looking at? Don't you know Paris?'

'Not very well. But the map's given me an idea. You know what? You'll see, we're going to have some fun.'

'Tell me, just the same.'

Sherazade was standing at the door. She'd read Pierrot's note, then she'd folded the bit of paper in four and put it in the inside pocket of her jacket. She wasn't going to mention it.

Oliver

They looked at Sherazade, wondering if she'd
really been crying. She stood there, looking for
all the world as if she'd just got up from a
salutary siesta, hardly a hair out of place. She
was smiling slightly.

'You've scoffed everything, you rotters. There
were two yoghurts left, I open the fridge, nothing.'

'It's Krim,' Basile said.

'Me? I ate the *harissa*.'

'Then it was Pierrot.'

'Yes, it was me . . . but I've got an idea for this
evening. It'll be brilliant. We're leaving in ten
minutes. We wear our balaclavas, tennis shoes
or trainers, all dressed alike, Basile as well, we're
not going out for a lark . . .'

'Stop bossing us around,' Basile said.

Pierrot explained what he'd got in mind for
them. They all fell in with his idea, Sherazade as

well, but she hadn't got a hood. Pierrot went and rummaged in Driss's cupboard; one day Driss had brought back a supply of the sort of balaclavas immigrants wear when working on building-sites or the roads. They'd all said, 'We're not Sonacotras;* we're not going to wear those things.' They didn't understand the purpose of such grotty woollen bonnets. Basile, in particular, would never have agreed to wear such a whatsit; he was absolutely crazy about all sorts of headgear that his pals, girls as well as boys, brought him that they'd found at the flea markets or in dustbins, he had quite a collection and every day he wore a different one. One day an African pal said, 'The only thing you haven't got is a tropical helmet.' The next day Basile walked into the kitchen wearing a white plastic tropical helmet. Pierrot promised to find him a genuine one that he'd seen in his mother's family, an uncle who'd spent some years in one of the French African colonies had brought it back, but in the North of France, the sun . . . Driss only had to put the balaclava on properly for them to understand what it could be used for. Eventually they all used them and each had his own which they wouldn't lend to anyone.

* Sonacotra – Société Nationale de Construction de Logements pour Travailleurs, body set up in 1963 for provision of housing for (immigrant) workers. The acronym adopted to refer, usually pejoratively, to the workers themselves. (Trans.)

Pierrot fetched a dark blue hood for Sherazade, who tried it on straight away in front of the mirror above the fireplace. This was very tarnished but she found a bit of glass that wasn't damaged. She could only see her eyes. Pierrot said, 'Sherazade's got green eyes.'

Krim looked at her. He hadn't noticed the colour of her eyes. Suddenly he exclaimed enthusiastically, 'Like my mother. My mother's a Berber, she's fair with light blue or green eyes, I'm not quite sure which. The next time I'll look more closely.'

Krim was slightly red-headed and had light-coloured eyes, more of a greyish-green. He always told Eddy he looked more like an Arab than he did; once the cops had stopped them in the Metro to check their papers, stopping Eddy first who was walking slightly in front. Eddy was born in Sarcelles to a Tunisian Jewish family.

Pierrot checked that Driss was still asleep. Eddy had gone out some time ago, no one knew if he'd be back. Basile picked up two large grey dustbin-liners and stuffed them inside his jacket, under his arm.

'Shall we take dark glasses?' asked Krim.

'We're not going sun-bathing . . .'

They went down to Pierrot's old Renault 4L. He said he'd found it in a cul-de-sac. It could have been true. Pierrot had an infallible system for opening locked vehicles and switching them on without a starting-key. Basile always asked him to look out for a really smart job, a BMW, a Porsche ... He replied, 'I don't come from Lyons, I've got no time for cowboys or roadhogs.' Basile called him a yobbo and a racist oik, which got Pierrot's goat and he told Basile to push off and shift for himself, like Krim who at least managed to pick up things he liked without bugging anyone. It was a fact that Krim had the knack of somehow or other laying his hands on magnificent bikes, powerful Japanese models. He'd passed his mechanic's diploma with distinction, but he couldn't stand having to obey a boss. He'd quit several good jobs. He read all the biking magazines and journals; he was given them or pinched them; he continued to improve his knowledge, taking stolen bikes to pieces and reassembling them in a secret outhouse he'd built at the bottom of the uncultivated garden of the house in the suburbs his father had managed to buy after fifteen years steady work at Renault's. Never absent, never ill, his father was considered a good worker and the foreman had recommended him for internal promotion. The house hadn't cost a lot. At the time there was a scheme for developing a ZUP* and the owners of

* *Zone à urbaniser en priorité* – priority urban development area. (Trans.)

the houses which were going to be demolished got a good price for them. The ones which were spared immediately depreciated in value, no one wanted to live near a ZUP which was going to house all the immigrants that the renovation of inner-city areas of Paris was driving out to the suburbs. Krim's father had first settled in Lyons. He'd sent for his wife and children. Krim was born in Lyons, then they'd gone to live in Grenoble and finally Paris where his father decided to stay when a cousin tipped him off about this affair. It was a good move. He didn't know whether he'd return to Morocco one day. He came from a village on the other side of the frontier. His wife was Algerian. They had met and married over there. She was very beautiful and flirtatious. She'd learned dressmaking in a sort of ladies' sewing circle and her husband, when he bought the house, had set aside a room for her to work at home. Orders were brought to her and she made them up at home. The father hadn't time to look after the garden; however he came from the country; he'd wanted to teach Krim to work the land, but Krim had always resisted. He loved city life and the suburbs. He didn't care for nature or country life. So he'd set up his workshop that no one entered at the bottom of this garden where nothing grew except the Arab parsley and mint that his mother cultivated near the kitchen, and there he stored Yammies and Kwakkers . . . He amused himself making new models on an empty frame. He drew them first and then tried to carry out his designs. He thought that one day he'd be famous for his new designs for bikes. For the moment, he got along.

Basile hoped the Renault wouldn't start. Then Pierrot would be forced to take another car, any other one. It started at the first turn of the key. Basile said, 'Shit!' and no one understood why.

Whenever Pierrot drove he began to sing at the top of his voice. He had a good voice but this habit never failed to irritate the 'users' as he called the people who travelled in his car. After a few minutes they all shouted, 'Shut up!' Pierrot kept quiet for a minute and a half and then started up again louder than ever.

'We're here,' Pierrot said. 'Look out!'

He stopped the car in a small dark street and left the doors unlocked.

'We meet again here, if you don't screw things up.'

Basile and Pierrot hadn't forgotten the .38 revolvers. They were not loaded. The could be mistaken for children's toy pistols.

Protected by a car, they kept watch on the entrance to the restaurant. Pierrot went down to the toilets, to look around. Not too small or too big. Very select. A restaurant where Oliver said he did the cooking himself. But as he owned a chain of Oliver's Restaurants he couldn't be everywhere at once. Pierrot didn't go to check whether Oliver was lending a hand in the kitchens. It smelt good. It was elegant and the waiters well trained. The *maître d*'s were not obsequious. The customers all wealthy middle-class. Pierrot had a pee and came back upstairs. Krim and Basile had peed behind the car while Sherazade was walking up and down. Pierrot returned.

'Remember! *This is an auto-reduction;* * it isn't a hold-up* . . . We can say that if we like, if we have the opportunity. Basile, you give one sack to Krim for the food and wine, one to Sherazade for the money, jewellery, watches. Put on the balaclavas. Good. Let's go.'

They went in, holding the .38s. Pierrot and Basile walked over to the head waiters.

'Don't move.' Pierrot kept the staff and the seated customers covered. Basile went round the tables with Krim and Sherazade. Krim took the unopened bottles; for the food it was difficult. Pierrot hadn't thought about the napkins and tableware but Krim tipped everything into his sack. Pierrot offered the waiters glasses of wine which they drank under the threat of the .38. He asked the proprietor for his cigars which he distributed among the bewildered waiters. Each

* This untranslatable expression derives from the extreme left-wing group in the 1970s, the Autonomes. They called thefts, burglaries, etc. for which they were responsible *'auto-réduction'*, claiming that they were returning to the poor riches which should have been theirs by right. (Trans.)

of them put the cigar into his waistcoat pocket. At one of the tables Basile recognized some people he'd met at one of his parties: none of them took him for Louis or Bob. Basile mercilessly made them empty their crocodile handbags and hand them over with money, jewellery, necklaces, bracelets, rings, earrings, signet-rings, watch-chains. Some of them hid their watches. Basile seized their wrists and recovered another dozen watches. Pierrot shouted that if any of them were students or were broke they could be let off. But they had to be quick. At the last table, near the door, Pierrot gave the signal, calling out, 'This isn't a hold-up; it's an auto-reduction.'

Krim and Sherazade were already running towards the car. Pierrot came out backwards, holding the .38 in his outstretched hand, Basile covered him from the door, his own .38 well in evidence so that no customer should get the idea of putting a chair or some other object in the way of Pierrot's retreat.

All four sat panting in the Renault for more than twenty minutes, hearts pounding, exhausted, not saying a word, their feet on the dustbin-liners.

'This is an auto-reduction,' Pierrot murmured.
'It isn't a hold-up,' replied Basile.

Meriem

Every day Meriem, Sherazade's sister, listened to messages broadcast from the independent radio stations, and looked at the personal ads in *Libération* and *Sans Frontière*, papers that her sister read regularly. She saw Anna-Maria at school but she still had had no letter from Sherazade. Every time the phone rang she rushed to answer it, for nothing.

Her mother asked her if she knew where her sister was, what she was doing, if she was going to see her. Meriem had no answer. Her mother wept, telling her daughter if Sherazade wanted to return she'd be pleased and so would her father. They couldn't understand why she'd left. She'd got everything she wanted. She didn't go out much, but she wasn't the only one, and her father's hidings weren't so terrible, after all.

That wasn't a reason.

Her father hadn't forced her into a marriage.

71

Several times he'd let her refuse a suggested match. And yet several of these would have satisfied her. The suitors had even said she could continue her studies at their expense; they offered good dowries; they had good jobs; some of them were in flourishing businesses. So why did she always say no? She'd got someone else? Their mother had put the question to Meriem. When she came home late after school, where did she go? Meriem kept telling her she went to the municipal library, but her mother couldn't believe her. Yet she knew that Sherazade read at night under the sheets with an electric torch. In the morning she found it under the mattress, with the batteries dead. Her mother couldn't stand seeing her reading like mad all the time when there was so much to do in the house with the younger sisters, but she always let her get on with her homework without disturbing her and she'd trained the little ones not to go into the bedroom where she was doing her prep.

And now Sherazade had disappeared in the middle of the year, just before taking her certificate exams. She was in her final school year.

Ever since she left, their father never stopped saying, 'She'd got everything at home, she'd got everything, what more did she want?'

Her elder brothers had searched for her. They'd gone to all the places where they heard that runaway Arab girls from immigrant housing estates congregated. They'd thought of everything, drugs, prostitution, but never of the library at Beaubourg. They'd gone to clubs where the hostesses were often said to be Algerian juveniles, nightclubs with Arab singers and dancers who looked like Egyptian girls in the Scopitones* in the Barbès and Jaurès neighbourhoods ... Scopitones for the Sonacotra who watched belly-dances, standing at the bar, with a half-pint in front of them, then another and yet another. The brothers had visited all the low-down joints as well as luxury clubs for wealthy Arabs in Paris on business. They'd actually seen girls who could have been their sister, but never Sherazade. They hadn't given up immediately. They didn't tell either of their parents about their nocturnal attempts to trace Sherazade. Meriem knew they hadn't found her. She told them to keep on. Their father never suspected these expeditions. Meriem had wanted to join in. Her brothers dissuaded her.

They now knew all the cafés and bars round the Gare du Nord, the Place de la République and the Champs-Elysées. They always went together. They didn't share out the work. The two of them preferred to do it together. There was one more trail which they hadn't yet followed up, clubs for Arab youngsters where they'd have found her if she'd been on drugs.

* *Scopitone*, the trade name of a sort of juke-box including a small screen, similar to that of a TV, on which is projected a film illustrating the music selected. (Trans.)

The eldest, who was articled to an accountant, found his money running out, he'd already spent a third of what he had left after handing over a sort of allowance to his father who never questioned him about what he did with his money. They had double expenses every time. It was ruinous. He said they'd have to stop after the Kiss Club, the Ponney Club and Mimi Pinson; they'd still go to the Nouba and the Gibus, even if Arab youngsters didn't meet there so often these days, or so they'd heard. They didn't go to clubs much themselves; they used to go to the Golf Drouot until it shut down. They preferred getting up parties with their own pals or going to Caribbean dances.

Every time, they asked, 'Would you by any chance have seen a girl with dark curly hair and green eyes?'

And they invariably got the same reply, 'Oh, you know, we see dozens of girls like that here, as for saying we've seen that particular one, we couldn't say for sure.'

'But she's got green eyes.'

'So what?'

'Well, you'd notice that, wouldn't you?'

'Oh, I never notice whether eyes are green, black, brown or blue, so it's no good asking me.'

They'd decided to leave a note for her at certain places where they thought there was a chance she might drop in. They'd put the same message on them all:

Sherazade, we are looking for you. Come home.

If you don't want to return, phone us.

Your brothers.

On the envelope they wrote her name SHER-AZADE. Often the waiter and the proprietor were illiterate and tried to decipher the name, screwing up their eyes with the effort, mangling it so that the brothers would repeat it in chorus, in order to cut short a painful scene, and the waiter and the boss would repeat it after them, after reading it again on the envelope.

'But what sort of a name's that? It's not from hereabouts,' French people who'd never heard of the famous *Arabian Nights* would say.

The brothers didn't reply. They'd thank them and go, leaving the waiter a handsome tip.

When the proprietor was an Arab or Kabyle, he'd take the envelope and give the brothers an understanding wink, as if to say, 'You can count on me.'

Two weeks later, the brothers had gone the rounds one last time of the cafés and clubs where they'd left the envelope for their sister. The letter was still there in every place, except in one bar in the Place de la République. But the proprietor was incapable of saying whether he'd lost it or if a girl who'd dropped in had taken it. He wasn't always in the bar and he wasn't always kept informed about everything. The letter wasn't

75

there. He would ask the waiters who were on duty. There were a great number of them and they worked in shifts; the bar closed very late, the staff came and went . . . the proprietor was repeating what the brothers had already realized; he couldn't make up his mind to question the waiters. Eventually the brothers found out that the first three had seen nothing, heard nothing, given nothing. Two of the waiters said they'd shown the envelope to a girl they'd seen and she'd taken it. One of them said she'd got black eyes; the other that they were green or blue, light-coloured in any case, he was sure.

From that day, the brothers waited for Sherazade's phone call as patiently as Meriem.

Julien Desrosiers

Julien Desrosiers was on his way back from the Drouot sale where he'd not found anything to suit his pocket. Orientalist pictures had been advertised, he'd read about it in *Le Monde* which gave the list of sales. He'd withdrawn money from his bank and rushed there immediately with the wad of notes all ready. He'd recognized the dealers in specialized pictures, antique-dealers, owners of Orientalist galleries. He knew he'd have no luck that day, especially when he saw an English collector turn up; knowledge-able, enthusiastic and a rich heiress into the bargain, she always snapped up everything. Julien attended the sale with an aching heart and a sick feeling. The banknotes that he fingered in his pocket seemed so paltry that he screwed them up into little balls and had trouble retriev-ing them later when he was looking for money to pay the grocer. He recalled portraits of Arab and

Berber women and children, Jewesses on their Moorish terraces, brides bathing, women of the harem . . . He thought he'd recognized a Chassériau . . . He was not mistaken. There were mutterings in the saleroom that this picture was not one of Chassériau's best . . . He would have been satisfied with it. It went to the English woman at a price which, while not reflecting the quality of the painting, was at least an indication of the rarity of a work, which inspired in Julien the same emotion as *Esther at her Toilet*, the subject being similar in its general composition to that of the picture Julien was very familiar with: a semi-nude white woman, waited on and celebrated by a Negress in a red and gold turban. He thought of Manet's *Olympia* that he often went to look at in the Jeu de Paume and which made him feel so uncomfortable, for some un-accountable reason. Perhaps on account of the coldness of the body, like a dead body beneath the knotted turban, whereas the head, in spite of its stiffness, touched him. He was moved by the gravity of the expression, the round earrings, the disproportionately small chin. The servant was also a Negro woman, black in the shadow of the nearly black curtain. She was presenting a sumptuous bouquet to her mistress. He told himself he must get rid of this strange trouble which made his heart beat faster every time he saw these two female figures in an Orientalist picture, so ubiquitous in Western nineteenth-

78

century painting, the one Black, the other White.

He completely forgot this artificial exoticism when he spotted Sherazade in her usual place. How had he managed to fall so quickly in love with a girl he didn't know, when he always maintained that he had never been in love? Was he lying? Had he forgotten? He was speaking the truth. He had never known love at first sight, until now.

He stopped to look at her.

Her face was turned three quarters towards him, bent over a book she was holding on her left knee which was crossed over her right leg.

He noticed her delicate round earings. An emerald set in gold. He'd never seen her wearing any jewellery, and suddenly he couldn't take his eyes off that brilliant green dot near a black curl behind her ear. From time to time, Sherazade pushed the curl back, touching the stone which was smooth as a pearl. Julien followed her movement, attentive and indiscreet, waiting for her to lift her head towards him, he'd moved slightly to force her to catch sight of him when she got tired of reading. But Sherazade just went on fingering her emerald and the tip of her left ear-lobe. Once or twice she scratched the top of her head hard, rumpling her hair over her forehead, without her noticing.

She was reading a book about the Algerian

War. The seat opposite Sherazade was occupied. Julien walked around the library, dipping into recent newspapers and magazines. He was waiting for a seat to be vacated, but he had to give up. He walked behind Sherazade, tore a sheet of squared paper out of his little spiral notebook in which he always took his notes and slipped it on the table; he had hurriedly scribbled, 'I'm in the bookshop, Julien.'

Soon, after he had already looked several times at all the books and albums laid out on the tables, Julien grew impatient. He decided he'd drop in at the library once more and then go home. He walked angrily towards the door with his head down and bumped into the glass pane. He heard someone burst out laughing near him and was just about to swear at the person when he saw it was Sherazade standing there with the headphones of her walkman round her neck in place of the red and yellow scarf she was wearing in the fast-food.

Driss

Sherazade was wearing Krim's biking jacket, the black one with gilt buttons. She liked it on account of its large number of pockets and because it was loose and lightweight. Krim took particular care of his biking gear. He had several outfits, black or red, leather or waterproofed cotton. He'd come back one day with a black cat-suit in soft leather, a studded jacket with an eagle on the back and a magnificent pair of biking boots. They'd all yelled with admiration and immediately asked what they'd cost. When Krim swore blind they cost half a million no one was surprised; he was talking in old francs, just like his parents. Everyone knew Krim had certainly not laid out a penny for this outfit that Sherazade said reminded her too much of traffic cops or SS officers. Krim told her she didn't know what she was talking about and became quite aggressive when she insisted although he wasn't usually violent. In the end he stormed out of the room with his helmet under his arm, saying, 'Fuck you, you stupid bitch,' and didn't speak to her again until she asked him to lend her his black jacket. They made it up. Krim was as keen as Driss on what they called their gear. Krim for the bike, Driss for town wear and chasing skirt. When Driss was occupying the bathroom of the squat, which Pierrot had restored and renovated, the others knew they'd have to wait a long time for it to be free. They protested and had to shave in the kitchen without a mirror or in front of the cracked mirror in the big room. When Driss emerged from the bathroom, his pals crowded round in admiration. 'Snazzy!' they exclaimed, repeating, 'Snazzy!' . . . then they all wanted to know where he'd found the whole rig-out, fingering the clothes while Driss recoiled from the assault. They examined him from head to toe – snazzy.

Basile counted on his fingers.

'How many birds are you going to bring back?'

'They won't be for you.'

'That's for sure.'

Basile pointed to Pierrot.

'Look how he's got up. You should give him some lessons, Driss.'

Pierrot retorted, 'Toy-boys aren't my scene . . .' and Driss took offence, though used to Pierrot's puritanical remarks, calling him the

'Stal', only knowing that this abbreviation of Stalin or Stalinist, as Basile had explained to him, was a political insult, but incapable of going further into its ideological implications, and with, 'Bye, everybody!' was off, slamming the door behind him. Sometimes he returned to the squat in the small hours with a couple of grand that he showed his pals; he'd played cards with other youngsters and not so young, Algerians and Moroccans, in places he'd never revealed the names and addresses of. Basile said, 'This time you didn't have to sell your jacket and boots.' As on a couple of occasions, in winter, Driss had found himself skint. He'd had to abandon his sheepskin jacket with the woollen collar and another one in waterproofed material, smooth as silk, lined with fur, 'Marmot, not rabbit,' he'd explained to the squat-mates. Basile asked him where he'd ditched his birds, his *muffs*; Driss let fly with invectives against Algerian girls who he called prick-teasers, and Basile reminded him of what one of their buddies had said who'd lived in the squat a few weeks before, 'I screw French girls, I don't touch Arabs, I leave them virgin for marriage, they're like my sisters,' and Driss replied he'd had a bellyful of French girls who had the hots for him, 'They're all crazy about me, dunno why . . .'

Basile burst out laughing. Repeated Driss's expression loud enough for the others to hear. He asked Sherazade and Djamila, 'You crazy about him?'

'No, no!'

'You see!'

Driss retorted, 'But they're Arabs . . .'

Djamila protested and Driss went on, 'Oh yes, that's right; Djamila's an adulterate.'

'What? What's that mean, adulterate?' Djamila shouted.

'Not pure Arab. You're half Arab, half French, it's quite clear!'

'OK. I thought you meant something else.'

'You see,' Driss said to Basile. 'Algerian girls are all depraved, and I'm not the only one to say so. Ask the others.'

Krim and Eddy were called, and Rachid if he happened to be there between two stays in DASS* hostels. Generally the argument ended there under some excuse or other. They didn't like this sort of talk in front of the girls, and besides they weren't sure how Sherazade and Djamila would react. Especially Djamila, as Eddy had told them she went on the game from time to time to buy smack. They didn't believe him. She didn't look like a junkie, they said, and they'd never seen her needing a fix like Driss. She managed things better.

* DASS – Department d'Action Sanitaire et Sociale, government organization, similar to British DHSS. (Trans.)

Djamila

Eddy had bumped into Djamila twice running, first at the Bastille, then at the Forum at the Halles; she looked as if she'd been drinking and was walking beside a well-dressed chap in a three-piece suit, fifty something, carrying a briefcase. She was talking loudly and laughing a lot; the second time, he'd followed her; he'd seen her go into a hotel in the neighbourhood and go upstairs with the man, then come down and say goodbye to him politely. She'd disappeared when he tried to find out where she went afterwards.

Sherazade already knew what Eddy revealed to his incredulous squat-mates. She was the only one Djamila talked to, often late into the night. She was waiting for letters from a fellow called Richard who she'd met in a queue at the Job Centre. She was alone in Paris. She disliked this city; she preferred Marseilles. She hardly ever left the room where Richard had put her up. He was an artist and the room was cluttered with canvases, cardboard boxes, pots of paint. He said he was a genius and he'd be recognized one day. Meanwhile he was living on the money his parents sent him from Lyons, the father was a company director, a member of the Socialist Party, he understood his son and tried to help him. Richard frequented the fashionable clubs. To earn a bit of money he worked in the trendy cafés around the Halles area. He served in the bar, but after three weeks the boss, an energetic smart young man, started to complain that he wasn't peppy or efficient enough, and when one day the rumour reached him that the fellows who hung around Richard were pushers who came to his place simply to contact him, he took the opportunity to tell him that this job didn't suit him and he could surely find something better and that the work was beneath him. He discreetly gave him his marching orders. Richard hadn't lasted long either at the Palace, or the Rex, clubs where he met the pals he'd tried to work with, who'd told him he'd got talent but never lifted a finger to try to find him a gallery to exhibit in, although they often knew gallery owners, art-dealers and a lot of wealthy patrons who liked to discover and help young artists, especially if they found them as attractive as their creations. When Djamila met Richard, he'd just left Annette, or rather Annette had left him, because she endlessly had to keep Richard supplied with food and art materials out of her modest salary as a nurse.

Djamila agreed to go home with Richard. He didn't force her to sleep with him and didn't keep an eye on her comings and goings. He didn't question her if she didn't come back till the morning when he was still asleep. Djamila said she'd found a job in a shoe shop in the Saint-Germain area, a smart boutique. She only stayed two weeks; she didn't like serving, still less kneeling down to help lazy stuck-up customers try on shoes they'd be quite capable of putting on by themselves at home; she had to unpack ten pairs of shoes for nothing, and at the end of the day the manageress told her, 'Djamila, you've not worked well today. You must be more obliging, you know. You don't smile, you look as if you're bored; the customers don't like that. They are particular about the quality of our goods and staff, so make an effort.'

Djamila thought she'd have liked to kill a couple of them, if she could, she knew which ones. When she'd seen the weapons in Pierrot's room, one day when he was cleaning them, she'd thought the .38 would do the job, but the next day she'd asked the owner for the money owing to her and went to see if it was not too late to register for the psycho course at the university – rather starve than sell shoes and having to put up with the smell of middle-class cows' feet – as she said to Richard who was tickled pink, though he realized they were broke now and that was no laughing matter. And so Djamila had hung around at the university, and as she couldn't find any training course she liked or if she did it only started in six months' time, as she was never satisfied with the jobs she was offered, chambermaid, telephonist, home help, when she'd got her *baccalauréat* ... true, she couldn't type, she started to let herself be picked up in the street, without ever having to take to street-walking or depend on a pimp, she found herself more than once in hotel rooms, always different ones as she didn't want to get known to the police or to the pimps. Richard had asked no questions about where the money came from that he used freely for his smack. Gradually Djamila had started using also and she said that at those times she felt good with Richard and she was more and more in love with him. He was lazy but he still painted, sometimes non-stop for hours on end. She watched him. She liked being there, watching Richard paint. It was restful after she'd been on a job when she'd had to argue with the punters when it came to paying up as they often tried to rip her off. She also tried to trick them out of having sex with her but it didn't always work and she got fed up with the perverts who didn't want to screw and asked her to beat them with wet towels or whips. She had to have money for clothes, she liked smart gear and giving presents to Richard who was capable of wearing the same pair of jeans for six months on end; she used her earnings to dress him to her taste. She found him all the more attractive.

Sherazade listened to her.

Camille or Rosa

Sherazade, too, had been propositioned fairly overtly and, more than once, she'd had to get up from the table or leave the club before the trap was sprung. She'd learned to judge the decisive moment very exactly. The men who invited her would never have thought her capable of such determination. They were astonished to see her suddenly harden, when they'd only got to the salad or the second whisky that she pretended to drink, a girl like her with her youthful, laughing face that had made them take an immediate fancy to her. Why did she suddenly turn nasty, coarse, vulgar, it didn't suit her . . . She'd listen to them murmuring these moral platitudes until she'd suddenly jump up, calling the man a disgusting old pig and a randy snake – it was Basile who had taught her this insult from Maoist Popular China – and then she'd stalk out stiffly before breaking into a run.

Some encounters had been more congenial. She was often picked up in phone boxes where you can see your neighbour through the glass panes. The man would signal to her and she'd choose whether to reply or not. When she knew there was nothing at the squat, in the fridge or in the cashbox and pockets had been turned out, and as she'd never descend to begging, if the bloke who tapped on the window of the call-box wasn't too repulsive she'd agree to have dinner with him, but never at his place. She preferred restaurants or big brasseries. One of them had taken her to the brasserie at the Gare de Lyon. She'd eaten well and laughed a lot. Before leaving he'd told her he worked as a stand-up comic, his job was to make people laugh. He wanted to see her again but she said he'd have to trust to luck and didn't give him her address or phone number. When asked what her name was she would either say *Camille* or *Rosa* according to the person. Pierrot had explained who Rosa Luxemburg was but she'd chosen this name before discovering that this Spartacist revolutionary was known as *Rosa Lux* – like light, added Pierrot, who knew everything about history and every revolution from Spartacus the gladiator and even before that. She liked listening to him in the evenings when the telly was on and the programmes didn't interest them. Basile also would get on his soapbox and hold forth about the history of the Negroes, the deportation, the slaves' revolts, starting first in Santo Domingo. Basile lent her books on Black Africa, the Caribbean, Toussaint L'Ouverture . . .

One evening Sherazade returned to the squat and burst in on them, interrupting their rehearsal. She'd had a narrow escape from two bastards in the Rue Saint-Denis. She needed to tell them about it.

'I'll point them out to you and you can bash their faces in, otherwise what's the good of going in for all that judo and karate and shooting practice in clubs like you do . . . So I was walking along in the Rue Saint-Denis, minding my own business . . .'

'And what the hell were you doing there? That street's no place for you.'

'I go where I want to, when I want to, and my place is everywhere.'

'All right, all right . . .'

'Exactly . . . OK, let me go on. I walk under a signboard. The place was empty. Two blokes come up to me, crowding me in and saying I can see the show for nothing if I like. I hadn't noticed where I was. I didn't suspect anything. I thought it was a cinema, I don't know what I thought. I went through the curtain with them and inside they jammed me in a little cubicle and forced me to watch. I saw a half-naked girl masturbating and smiling. I shut my eyes. I didn't know she couldn't see me. I twigged where I was. I struggled like mad, I yelled, the

92

girl behind the one-way mirror went on, the blokes told me, "Look at her, you little bitch, get an eyeful and see that you take it in, 'cos you're going to be put behind the mirror like her, you'll earn a heap and us too." They pulled my hair to make me look up. I screamed and bit and kicked. They heard a noise, a customer perhaps, and they let go and I ran off . . .'

'You see . . . that's no place for you, I told you so.'

'Never go alone in that area. That's all.'

Sherazade was furious and swore at them.

'Is that all you've got to say . . . Those two bastards could have raped me and you stand here . . .'

'They raped you?'

'No.'

'So, you see . . .'

'I see, I see what? I see you don't understand anything. You talk big, that's all.'

'What d'you want us to do?'

'I dunno. At least say they are bastards, scum.'

'OK. They're bastards, scum, rotters . . .'

Sherazade walked out and shut herself in the bathroom. After an hour Krim came and banged on the door. 'Sherazade!' She wouldn't answer. Krim said he was going to break the door down. 'Just try.' Krim said, 'Good, you haven't committed suicide, so that's all right.'

In the evenings, when Djamila talked about herself, Sherazade said, 'Djamila, you say you don't like working for a boss or waiting on customers but these blokes, they make use of you, OK? You do what they ask you to, you're working for them.'

'No. I make use of them. I give them a blow job. I take their dough.'

'But you don't take it for nothing, you satisfy their kinky fancies with your body.'

'I'm telling you, I make use of them, and if you want to know, I think that girls who sleep with blokes for free are sluts who give themselves for nothing and haven't even thought their bodies are worth something and the blokes must cough up if they want them, you understand?'

'No.'

'OK. Drop it. It's not worth trying to explain to you.'

Sherazade asked Djamila to tell her about Richard. Djamila told her she was waiting for him. He'd gone off one morning, leaving a note on the pillow. 'I'm leaving for Thailand on business. I'll be rich and you too. Wait for me. Richard.'

She'd had no word from him for three months. She didn't know what he was doing or why he'd left like that, without warning. She thought the police might be after him. She added that she wanted to break if off, she was fed up with it all, it was a bad scene, and turning tricks . . . she

94

was going to get shot of all that and attend lectures properly at the university ... Several times she'd made herself similar promises that she'd never kept. This time she really meant it, she promised Sherazade. She'd go back soon to Marseilles. Her sister wrote to her in Paris, *poste restante*, to say she'd be welcome to share her two-room flat and she'd find her a job where she worked. She wouldn't wait for Richard. Besides, she'd soon be going to Algeria.

'Me too,' said Sherazade.

Vanves

'You coming to my place?' Julien said to Sherazade at the door of the bookshop.

'If you like.'

'Those are super earrings you've got. The same green as your eyes.'

'Yes. That's what Pierrot says.'

'Who's Pierrot?'

'A buddy.'

Suddenly Julien was no longer keen to take Sherazade home with him. She'd scarcely said a word but he didn't feel like it any more. He'd have left her standing there; he'd have broken into a run and vanished. Sherazade was looking at him. He gave up the idea of running away.

Julien was preparing avocados in the kitchen and cutting mangoes in two. He wondered if Sherazade liked kiwis and even if she'd ever eaten them. He rinsed the lamb's lettuce and took out a bottle of bordeaux. He switched on the radio. He swore because he couldn't get France Musique on account of all the independent radio stations whose wave lengths were so close. He switched off Rock Boulevard on 92.6 MHz and went to put on a record in the room next to the kitchen. He chose *Siegfried.*

'D'you like Wagner?'

'Who's he?'

'Listen, that's Wagner, Richard Wagner. A German.'

Sherazade had taken off her tight red shoes and was sitting in the wicker armchair, rubbing her feet, near the round table which Julien was going to lay.

'D'you like kiwis?'

'What's that?'

'You'll see. They're delicious.'

'Where they come from?'

'A very long way.'

Sherazade got up, took off the biking jacket and threw it on the bed in the corner of the room next to the white wooden bookcases. She was wearing a red shirt, like the ones worn by the Southerners in the American Civil War and she'd turned a flap back on the left. She fingered the delicate gold chain she'd worn ever since the evening when they'd shared out the spoils. When Pierrot tipped the contents of the dustbin liner out on to Sherazade's red bedcover, they'd all shouted in chorus, 'Wow!' and Pierrot said, 'This isn't a hold-up,' and Basile, 'It's a miracle!'

They'd all fallen on their knees beside the bed, anxious to plunge their hands into the glittering heap, but not one of them put a hand out. Sherazade, as dazzled as they were, carefully sorted everything into piles, watches, necklaces, dress rings, signet rings, earrings. Then she'd separated the jewellery and watches into: Women, Men.

Pierrot said, 'We'll let Sherazade choose,' and he offered her the pair of emerald earrings.

'You've got pierced ears and you never wear anything in them.'

'I left mine at home. An aunt in Algeria gave them to me before I left for France, I was three I think.'

'You like them?'

'Yes.'

Sherazade also took a solid gold chain to wear round her neck, a plain gold keeper ring and an antique ring. She never wore a watch and what she chose she'd keep. When they'd each taken whatever they fancied, the rest would be sold to the fences that Krim knew over at Montmartre. Krim thought about his French girlfriend, Pierrot took some ladies' jewellery which he intended for Sherazade. Driss and Basile chose signet rings, gold watches and chain bracelets. Driss had woken up just in time to take part in the share-out from the raid. He put an antique watch on one side for Eddy who collected them.

After the remaining jewellery had been sold,

the proceeds were shared out equally. Pierrot said they had to keep some pieces for a rainy day. They found a hiding place that they all swore never to reveal. As for the table napkins and the silver cutlery, they decided it would be nice to eat with such fine tableware, so each of them would be entitled to their own set. They put a dozen of each on one side, the rest would be flogged at the flea market, together with the napkins that they wouldn't keep as they'd have to be washed and ironed, and nobody would do that.

So, one Sunday morning, Pierrot, Basile and Sherazade, the others were still asleep or had left, went off to the poorest flea market so as not to risk being spotted by specialist second-hand dealers who might have heard of the Oliver affair. They each squatted down in front of their box of goods that they sold to antique-dealers and foreign tourists. Sherazade's box was empty. Early on she had swopped two table napkins for a pair of black harem pants from the woman selling next to her, she was eating a *merguez* sandwich and chips, when Pierrot saw her suddenly run for it and disappear.

'What's up with her?'

'Who?' asked Basile.

'Sherazade, she's vanished.'

'Leave her . . . You hang around her a bit too much.'

'Me? Hang around her? Just say that again . . .'

Pierrot yelled.

'Yes, you hang around her.'

'You think so. Really?'

'It's too bloody obvious. Just look out.'

'Why?'

''Cos she'll land you in the shit.'

'That's not so sure.'

'You'll see.'

'You jealous or what?'

'Me? Jealous? That'll be the day . . .' Basile burst out laughing and went on, 'If she tells you she's in love with you, then I'll be jealous, but now . . . has she said she's in love with you?'

'No,' Pierrot said softly.

'So, you see. I'm telling you you're hanging round her too much.'

'Shall we go and look for her?'

'No.'

When they got back to the squat, Sherazade wasn't there. Pierrot decided to go and look for her. Basile told him not to be a bloody fool.

'Where are you going to look? You've no idea where she might be.'

'That's true.'

'We never know where she goes when she leaves here, so what's the use?'

'It's not so complicated. We just have to hang around Saint-Michel, Bastille, République, the Halles, always the same places, Strasbourg-Saint-Denis, all those places.'

'You go by yourself, I'm staying to watch TV.

Don't forget the meeting this evening; we've got some important decisions to take, and tomorrow we're rehearsing with Eddy ... If she comes back before you, what do I tell her?'

'Nothing. Don't say I was looking for her. Right?'

'OK. Right.'

That evening, Sherazade met Zouzou and France.

She'd run off because she'd thought she recognized her parents and her little sisters in the distance. She'd forgotten that the flea markets constituted the regular Sunday-morning outing for immigrant families. But her family usually went to Montreuil. Why had they decided on Vanves that morning?

Feraoun

At Julien's place, Sherazade looked at the wall hung with little pictures. She'd put the headphones of the walkman on again. Her earrings were no longer visible. She swayed to the rhythm of music inaudible to Julien. She was wearing the black toreador pants from the flea market that Josiane had chosen for her. 'You're slim, they'll fit you, they're a small size 36 or 38.'

The phone rang.

Julien carried on a long conversation while Sherazade walked around the room, stopping to look at some of the books on the shelves; she'd recognized some by Algerian writers that she'd read in the Municipal Library at Aulnay-sous-Bois, recommended by the librarian, a warm jolly young woman who thought of her as soon as she read an article or a new book arrived on North Africa. Just because Sherazade had once asked for a book by Mouloud Feraoun that her grandfather had told her about when she'd gone to stay for an extended holiday in the little village in Eastern Algeria, where the writer came from, and where she'd stayed for nearly the whole school year with her sister Meriem, at her maternal grandfather's who'd been a teacher at the Qur'anic school and could read and write French – he used to write letters for the families of men from the village who'd emigrated to France.

When she read the form that Sherazade had filled up to get her reader's ticket, the librarian realized she'd be able to lend Sherazade, who would read them, certain books that she, the librarian, had bought and catalogued, books that French people never read because they didn't know about them or because anything that didn't belong to their national heritage didn't interest them. She'd had to keep completely up to date, as Sherazade read quickly, returned the books punctually and always asked for more. Besides more and more girls from North African immigrants' families came to the library, and not only to escape from their parents' supervision. It was a place to meet, where they would chat, read, help each other choose books, dip into newspapers and some of them had suggested subscriptions to *Libération* and *Sans Frontière* as they didn't read *L'Humanité* or *Le Monde*. They'd also asked for magazines and they'd been provided for them.

''Bye Enrico. See you tomorrow.' Julien rang off.

Sherazade was standing near the window looking at a watercolour that she'd taken down. It depicted an Arab woman with a baby in her arms. A woman from the south, a Berber most likely, not wearing a veil.

'You like it?'

'Yes.'

'Would you like it?'

'Dunno.'

'You can have it if you like, I'll give it to you. I very nearly didn't get it. One Saturday morning I went to the flea market in Montreuil. I walked round several times and spotted this woman. There were other watercolours by the same artist, but I liked this one. It cost quite a lot and I hadn't any cheques on me that day. I kept my eye on it until I had to leave, and I told myself I'd go back and buy it the next day. On Sunday, I got up early and went back to the place where I'd seen this picture the day before, and it had gone. I asked the dealer and he said he'd sold it last thing Saturday evening. I was miserable and felt prepared to buy anything as long as it had an Algerian woman . . . An Arab woman.

'But why are you so keen on all those women?'

'I love them.'

'You love pictures of them?'

'Yes, that's right . . . Let me finish. You don't find portraits of women every Sunday at the

Montreuil market. I wandered around without seeing anything, then suddenly, I felt she was there . . . I looked up. I was quite right. The watercolour had been bought by another dealer who knew the first one. He was asking twice as much for it. My knees were shaking. It was the same picture all right, with the price marked double that of the previous day. I bargained with the dealer, explaining what had happened. He was busy selling a very fine Napoleon III dinner service to some Germans. He did well out of it so he lowered the price of the watercolour and I took it home without even a glance at it. When I got home I took off the newspaper it was wrapped in; I cleaned the glass with spirit and put the picture in front of the books before hanging it on the wall with the others. You can choose, if you want another one. Take anything you like.'

They'd nearly finished eating. Julien had switched Wagner off some time ago, and at the same time Sherazade had put her walkman down on the edge of a whatnot.

The phone rang.

It was Enrico again, asking if he could drop in to see a Godard or an American film that evening at Julien's. Julien had a video and nearly all his favourite films. He also recorded programmes on TV that he couldn't see when he was working. In his bedroom, near his desk, he had a computer that he'd managed to buy cheap. He didn't explain all that to Sherazade, he knew she'd be bored.

'No, I don't feel like watching a film this evening, you know. I think I'll go out; we can meet at the Rex if you like. It's Thursday, so I'll see all the other chaps . . . I've not seen for a long time . . . 'Bye for now!'

Sherazade thought the kiwis 'really, really t'riff'; she ate them all. Julien didn't want any, he preferred the mangoes which Sherazade left for him .

'Where d'you sleep? Here?' Sherazade asked.

'No, I've a bedroom next door and at the end I've set up a lab for my photography. It's a very big room, with a double bed.'

'You've got a wardrobe?'

'No.'

'In my mother's bedroom, there was a big wardrobe, huge, it went right up to the ceiling. She put everything in it. We're nine in the family, we each had a drawer with our name on and our own colour. Mine was red. My mother hid her jewellery in a false bottom. I knew where it was. Jewellery she'd brought from Algeria, some that my father had bought for her here. Arabs like gold and the women like jewellery. When I left, I took my mother's jewellery. In case I needed money . . . I've still got it all. I'm holding on to it. I don't wear it, I don't sell it. Perhaps one day . . .'

Julien spent part of the night at the Rex.

Sherazade didn't want to go. Julien told her to slam the door behind her when she left.

Eddy

Eddy turned up just in time for the encounter. He'd recognized Djamila from a distance. What was she doing in the middle of this scuffle and screams that could be heard from level four? He rushed up to the group. Djamila, who was bigger than the other girls, had spotted Eddy and was waving to him frantically while she continued to struggle with a punk who was raining punches on her. This girl, the leader of a gang, was strolling about the Forum with her hangers-on, brandishing bicycle chains and amusing herself spitting on suburban sightseers and other people. A gob of spit, probably not aimed at her, had landed on Djamila, who hadn't waited to find out the truth about the girl's intentions; she'd flown at her and they began to fight with a violence that Eddy would never have suspected the first time he saw Djamila at the squat. Eddy was about to intervene, because Djamila was outnumbered and was beginning to weaken, when the commotion around them indicated a bunch of cops arriving at the double.

The punks, who were probably all juveniles, ran off towards the escalators but Djamila had to show her papers. They were in order. She was not a minor. She went off with Eddy in the opposite direction to the punks.

Djamila hadn't noticed how attentive Eddy had become to her since she'd been sharing Sherazade's room at the squat. As she was still thinking about Richard, she hadn't taken the trouble to look at Eddy. He was a pal. In the streets around the Halles, she had the impression she was seeing him for the first time. As Driss said, he looked more Arab than himself.

'Where you from?'

'Sarcelles.'

'You sure?'

'I was born in Sarcelles, my parents are Tunisian, Tunisian Jews; they'd been living there for generations. My grandparents still speak Arabic. They've got a shop in Belleville. You'd like to go there? It'll be a change.'

The grandfather sat them down, gave them Tunisian cakes and a glass of tea . . . It was in Rue Ramponeau, where they passed as many squads of cops as isolated pushers, that Eddy realized his blunder. He'd come with Djamila to just the wrong place. Djamila didn't say anything. They went back to the Metro without a word.

'I'm going back,' Djamila said.

'So'm I . . . You know, Djamila, I've been thinking, s'pose we went to Tunisia. My parents have never been back and I don't know their country. It's a bit my country too and then, Algeria is just nearby and we could go on there . . . Would you like to?'

'Yes. Why not.'

Eddy kissed her on the neck. Djamila didn't push him away. Suddenly she fancied him.

Back at the squat, they found Pierrot and Krim kneeling on the floor, looking at a map of the outskirts of Paris.

'What the hell are you doing on all fours?'

'You can see. We're looking at a map of the Paris suburbs,' Pierrot said. 'You know our group publishes a paper called *The Suburbs are Fine*'

'I'd no idea. I knew about *Rock Police Against* and the paper for the Lyons girls *Zâama*, but not *The Suburbs are Fine*, no. I've never even seen it mentioned in the *Agit'Presse* ads in *Libé*.'

'You never see anything. That's why. Anyway, piss off. We're busy.'

Pierrot hadn't seen Sherazade for several days. He'd got a job as a courier for a super cool magazine, and he hadn't got time to go and look for her. He'd written her a long letter and put it on her red bedcover, where she couldn't miss it, but every morning when he glanced through the half-open door he saw the envelope with her

110

name *Sherazade*. He'd written several, one a day, with a different name every time: *Rosa*, *Kahina*, *Olympia*, *Suzanna*, *Leïla*, *Roselane*, mixing up, unknown to Sherazade who'd never heard of any of these famous women, the revolutionary, the prophetess and warrior, the odalisque, the member of the Italian Red Brigade, the Arab poetess, the Turkish Sultana . . . In this way he forgot to be miserable. Basile was right, he'd really been hanging round her too much. Pierrot had also cut out for Sherazade messages that appeared in *Libé*. Messages signed *Meriem*. The same message that appeared nearly every day. She must have seen them but Pierrot still put them next to the letters, in the order of their appearance. The sub-editor in charge of the ad pages had entered them under the heading *Arabian Nights,* printed in bold type; Pierrot had left the heading which he thought dreadfully corny.

Bobigny

Sherazade reappeared the day set for them to do a break-in in Bobigny. She went to her room, picked up the letters and the ads which she put with a few items of clothing in the overnight bag slung across her shoulder.

Pierrot was so upset he couldn't speak; it was Krim who called out to her; anyway she wasn't meaning to leave again immediately. She was keen to see them.

'You coming with us?'

'Where to?'

'Bobigny.'

'What for?'

'We'll explain. Pierrot knows that area well, he's shown me on the map. He's got a buddy in Bobigny. They've done a recce. There's an isolated house. The owners often go away for the weekend. It's a rich place. Everything's set. You'll hold the shooter. Krim'll stand guard;

Mouloud and Pierrot know their jobs. We mustn't forget the gloves, we won't need the balaclavas. Mouloud's brother got nicked on account of finger-prints . . . Pierrot says that if this comes off, next time he'll do a hold-up, it brings in more: he says his group needs dough, more than we do . . . He'll do it by himself or with Basile . . . I couldn't give a fuck for their group . . . So what about it?'

'It's bloody silly, I've just found a job. A shop where they sell super togs. You should just see. In the Halles. You feel like taking the lot.'

'We can do a stick-up job there too.'

'No way.'

'If you say so. You coming?'

'You'll take me on your bike? The Yammi?'

'Yes, if you like.'

'Afterwards, you can teach me to ride. It's easier outside Paris.'

Pierrot prepared the tools, pistols, gloves . . . map, they'd study it in a café together with the sketch plan that Mouloud had drawn on the spot of the house, the surrounding streets, the waste ground.

'If anything goes wrong,' Pierrot remarked, tapping the map, 'there's a cemetery nearby. It's even a Muslim cemetery, Krim, you hear that? And you too, Sherazade, that's just for the two of you, 'cos I want to be cremated, I've already let my folks know, they're Communists, so they agree.'

113

'What you saying all that for? It's dangerous?'

'It's always dangerous. Let's go.'

The owner of the house was crazy about electronics. He'd got everything you can think of in the way of the most sophisticated equipment. Pierrot and Mouloud were dazzled. They couldn't carry everything. 'We'll take the latest models and come back for the rest,' said Mouloud, sick at having to leave all these things, polished, tidily stored, labelled. Sherazade held the pistol like in the films, firmly without wavering. She told the lads not to talk so loudly and to hurry up. They kept saying, 'We can't leave that, we can't.' There was no money or jewellery to be found.

Mouloud opened a cupboard and screamed so loud he frightened Pierrot and Sherazade.

'Belt up!' Pierrot said.

'Come and see, come and see.'

Pierrot and Sherazade looked in the cupboard which he'd flung wide open. That was where the cop kept his uniform, immaculate. Mouloud saw the riot helmet, the kepi. He looked for the riot shield but couldn't find it and took the truncheon.

'That really makes me fucking mad, Pierrot, you've seen that . . . I could die . . . wait.'

He went to the kitchen and came back with a serrated carving-knife and a pointed bread-knife. He set about ransacking the place. In the garage he'd spotted an axe, he used it to smash

114

the furniture which was tough. He tore down
the curtains, smeared the walls, split open the
armchairs and couch, in the bedroom he over-
turned the bed, the chest-of-drawers and the
cop's wife's dressing-table, whose mirrors shat-
tered against the wardrobe. Pierrot tried to stop
him. He was making a row, it was all going to be
screwed up, all because of that uniform, it was
too stupid. He knew that Mouloud had done
time, after years in care from where he'd always
run away. The cops had ill-treated him, insulted
him . . . He wouldn't stop, if Pierrot would just
leave him alone. Mouloud took a pair of scissors
and cut the uniform into almost even strips, the
shirt as well and pierced holes in the kepi. He
wanted to keep the riot helmet – as a souvenir –
but Pierrot forced him to leave it behind and
threatened to bash his face in if he didn't leave
immediately with him.

Sherazade shoved the pistol in his back for a
joke, but Mouloud was so shaken that he put his
hands up. This grotesque gesture brought him
down to earth again and the realization of the
risks they were all running, after they'd wrecked
the house and murdered the cop's ghost.

When they passed the Muslim cemetery that
he'd shown Sherazade on the map of the outskirts of Paris, Pierrot slowed down and said to
Mouloud, 'You nearly sent us all there . . . You
can thank God, if you believe in him.'

Instinctively, Mouloud, whose mother had

taught him the *fatiha* when he was a kid and still spoilt him because he was the only boy, began to recite the prayer, although he always said to anyone who'd listen to him that he didn't believe. However he found himself having more and more discussions with his former pals from the shanty-town who had suddenly become Muslims; they said their faith brought contentment and it's true that when he talked to them now they gave an impression of such serenity, such amazing happiness that he got worried about himself. Were they out to convert him? He resisted, but he still went out of his way to meet them because it did him good to listen to them and they taught him a lot. It was the first time anyone talked to him about the Qur'an. They explained it to him. They told him the history of the Arabs, of Islam . . . He no longer felt humiliated because his father collected the French people's shit and he and his brothers had been seen on the estate in handcuffs.

'Mouloud! What's eating you?'

'Nothing. I'm thinking.'

'Oh! fine! What about?'

'I'm just thinking, that's all . . . with this job, it's all over.'

'What is?'

'Break-ins, hold-ups, all that, I've had a bellyful.'

'It's because of the cemetery and God that you're saying that?'

'Dunno. Perhaps.'

Pierrot's Peugeot, a 504 estate car, was piled full to the roof. They had to drive fast as the load could attract attention. They went straight to the fence's depot. Pierrot exchanged some of the cameras for light arms and false identity cards. Basile had left to spend two or three weeks in Guadaloupe, stopping over in Martinique for some contacts. Pierrot waited for him to return to tell him about this job.

Julien Desrosiers

Sherazade had gone to bed in the big room, near the phone. She'd put the watercolour on the Chinese table beside the bed. She had to be at the dress shop at nine o'clock the next morning, in the Halles, where she'd gone the previous day with Zouzou. She'd dropped asleep straight away, in her T-shirt, with her clothes chucked all anyhow on the carpet at the foot of the bed. She'd folded her bra and panties and taken care to hide them under her slacks before getting into bed.

Julien stumbled over one of Sherazade's shoes in the doorway. He switched on the light. She was there. He began to whistle softly as he removed his jacket and Palestinian scarf.

Sherazade was asleep.

The shutters had not been lowered. It must be five o'clock. Julien looked at his watch and hummed, 'It's five o'clock and Paris is waking

118

. . . It's five o'clock and I'm not sleepy . . .' and immediately broke into the song that was on everyone's lips at that time, '. . . *five a.m. and I'm wide awake, my teeth are chatt'ring, I shiver and shake, I turn up the sound . . . In the rumpled blue sheets, in bed all alone, I toss and turn, can't get to sleep . . . I begin to panic, cigs all gone . . . I've run out of Kleenex and nothing to drink . . .*' Julien had even bought the record: the song was called *Chagrin d'amour.*

Sherazade was asleep. Sherazade was there. He gazed at her. It was nearly light. He didn't need to switch on the light in the room. He was born in 1953, one year before the Algerian War, he would soon be thirty, how old was she? He'd no idea. She hadn't said much up to now . . . Her mother's wardrobe, that's all . . . he couldn't even remember how that had come up. She must be the eldest girl of a large family and most probably Algerian, if that was her real name. He could be twice her age. He gazed at her; from the end of the bed she looked fifteen. And himself . . . Suppose she was under age? He hadn't thought of that. Standing next to the sleeping Sherazade he was suddenly struck by the incongruity of this affair. He remembered what she'd said when she talked of her mother's wardrobe. At five in the morning, sitting in the wicker armchair, facing the sleeping girl, it dawned on him. 'Shit! Shit and shit again!'

He shut himself in his bedroom and put on

Mahler's *Lieder*. He felt like hearing a woman's voice, Frederica von Stade's voice. He turned up the volume. Too bad if it woke her up. He wasn't sleepy.

It was nearly midday when Julien woke. He hadn't any work appointments. In the bathroom he remembered Sherazade. The bed had been made, nothing was lying around, no sign of her presence, as if no one had been there. He simply noticed the watercolour was on the Chinese table. He shaved, got dressed without washing, cleaned his teeth, didn't bother with coffee or orange juice and rushed to the library. He asked one of the regulars if he'd seen a girl about seventeen, dark, curly hair, green eyes, wearing a biking jacket with gilt buttons, she came there fairly often, he'd have recognized her. The reader snapped back that he didn't come here to pick up birds, was he expected to notice every bit of skirt . . . Julien went to the fast-food. On his way back to Beaubourg he remembered he'd forgotten to switch on his answer-phone. He hadn't even given Sherazade his number. What a stupid clot!

He didn't live far away. He left a note for Sherazade on the door, simply giving his phone number. If she was passing. If she felt inclined . . . He had to consult some rare books at the Bibliothèque Nationale. He went on with his research till the library closed. He was told he would find certain books in the Library of the

Institute of Oriental Studies where he was quite at home since deciding to learn Arabic, after two years' post-graduate studies in Aix-en-Provence. His parents would have liked to see him register at the University of Bordeaux, but Julien preferred Provence to the Bordeaux region. He hadn't even asked Sherazade if she spoke Arabic. He liked the idea of talking to her in Arabic; perhaps she'd be more talkative in her native tongue? He promised himself he'd surprise her. He'd spent several months in a *medresa* in Cairo and went to all the Egyptian films, just like the immigrant workers that he met in the special cinemas where they only showed films in Arabic. Perhaps Sherazade wouldn't like his accent. When he'd travelled in North Africa for his studies, going from Morocco to Tunisia, he'd noticed that the Arabs pretended not to understand him. Eventually he'd had to familiarize himself with the Maghreb demotic and when he arrived in Tunisia they didn't make fun of him any more and took him for an Algerian. He was working simultaneously with the colonial archives and those of Arabic literature and Arab civilization. When he talked about this, people were always surprised that he took the same interest in such different works – so antagonistic – as they said. But these contradictions, if they existed, didn't worry him. He was curious about everything that constituted the most distant history, that of his own people,

121

and that of two peoples, two civilizations who have been in close contact from the time of the Crusades. Julien was planning to travel in the Maghreb and the Middle East and search for ancient and modern manuscripts that he knew existed and which he'd promised to find for Sinbad Publications. He'd managed to obtain videos of Arabic films that he intended to show Sherazade as well as some American films, and the Godards and Eustaches that he was sure she hadn't seen.

He liked sophisticated machines, he was interested in robots, but at the same time he was crazy about old manuscripts, libraries, archives. When he talked about these things to his mother, she was worried.

'But you're forgetting the other things, my boy.'

'What other things?'

'Books, machines . . . cinema. All that, pictures, museums, libraries . . . There are other things in life.'

'Of course!'

'You say you're all alone . . . I don't understand.'

'Because I live alone, is that it?'

'No. You know very well. I often talk about this to your father. He thinks the same as me.'

Before going to the cinema, Julien bought some cheeses and a pineapple. He'd go home as late as possible. When he saw the note on the door and recognized it as the one he'd put there that morning, he nearly left again. He would phone Enrico, his friend from Oran who he'd met again in Aix-en-Provence, then in Paris, a Jew whose family had been living in Tlemcen, then in Oran ever since the Spanish Inquisition. They often argued about points of history concerning the Jews, Arabs and Berbers in North Africa. They had nearly fallen out over the Kahina. Enrico maintained that she and her people practised the Jewish religion, Julien laughed at this legend. Enrico had said he would do some research on this and Julien would have to give in. They sometimes ran into each other at the School of Oriental Studies or the BN. Julien teased Enrico about his research which never seemed to advance. Apart from Ibn Kaldun's writings, all the rest was airport romances; he ought to go to Algeria, into the Aures mountains . . . the Algerian and Overseas archives had not been exhaustively studied . . . Perhaps he would be in luck. Enrico worked in computors. He did business deals and was interested in everything to do with North African Jews and Arabs. He personally subsidized research and fringe magazines that were beginning to make a name. He told Julien that in two or three years he would set up a Judeo-Arab Press.

Julien did not go to Enrico's. He watched an Egyptian film with Farid al-Attrach. He was not sleepy. About two in the morning he went for a

123

walk round the Halles and Beaubourg; he looked at the few passers-by, as if he might see Sherazade.

Zouzou and France

He had no idea that, at that very moment,
Sherazade was with Zouzou and France, who
worked with her in the dress shop in the Halles,
'letting her hair down', as Zouzou put it, at a
party they'd been invited to by a wealthy sup-
plier to the boutique. The two of them, Zouzou
and France, often went together to these crazy,
extravagant parties where the champagne
flowed and which gangs of youngsters gate-
crashed the first time they went, and were
accepted and in demand at afterwards, providing they were attractive and amusing. They
weren't required to have brilliant university
careers or be well connected. They were invited
for themselves, for the charm and grace they
exhibited when they danced and chatted, when
they put themselves out to please. They knew
how to be the life and soul of a party. They were
good fun. The new yuppie circles, with their

good education and excellent taste, were prepared to let themselves be exploited, for one evening, by these crazy, cocky, captivating young things, most of whom were born in the concrete jungle of the suburbs. They had nearly all been involved at some time or other in the petty crime or major criminal activities common to their native housing estates. They were fascinated by the outward signs of everything up-to-date, always attracted by anything flashy, but sufficiently critical to wear or use it with their tongues in their cheeks; they went in for everything that came directly from the USA, music, electronics, clothes, but were choosy and the label 'Made in USA' was not enough. They scrounged and ferreted and rooted around, succeeding, each in their individual way, in being absolutely with-it, if not actually setting new trends. Dress-designers' eagle eyes could immediately pick them out at these parties and fashion photographers always chatted them up, in the hope of getting them to pose for photos which would be the inspiration for inexpensive ready-mades which would sell well. These gangs of outlandish young things might herald a new craze, they mustn't be neglected, you never know, you must stay in the swing – and when your job involved display, the social comedy, society games, it was essential to keep your eyes open. It was exciting to have them around to look at; they weren't as dirty as the punks who'd been haunting these parties at one time, and they didn't drink so much beer: there was no risk of them flinging bottles at the high windows of the warehouses transformed by talented architects into magnificent residences with interior gardens, fully grown palms and luxurious fountains. The gangs travelled from oriental palaces to modern-style minimalist flats, with bare floor and walls and no furniture, or just one huge natural leather couch and a few mirrors. One of these gangs had once spent the evening at an eighteenth-century town house, so elegant that for several days afterwards when they met in the fast-foods when there were no parties at private houses or at the clubs currently all the rage, they had reminded each other of all the valuable objects and pictures by great masters. One of them suggested a burglary, which would save him two years apprenticeship as an electrician, 'Don't count us in,' retorted the others who didn't want to give up their evening parties where the luxury made them forget hours spent in queues at job centres, hours standing in shops at the Forum, hours spent in the sickening smell of hot croissants and tarts which they sold non-stop to commuters on the RER. They didn't complain, they didn't bemoan their lot; they had fun; they took everything in, sharpening their wits and all their senses at these parties as they paraded and showed off for a joke but not only. Some of the gang were amateur photographers, others drew comic strips. The best-looking among them hoped at least once to make such a stir that a cinema director, a photographer, an advertising agent, would suggest giving them a trial part, taking a series of fashion photographs, employing them as models ... It had been known to happen. Why not to them?

Zouzou and France were always with the gang, especially on Friday and Saturday evenings. They had dragged Sherazade along with them, when she hadn't felt like going back to the squat, nor to Julien's, too early in the evening. They didn't wear fancy-dress, but Zouzou and France got themselves up so as to attract attention. The owner of the boutique let them wear a selection of clothes which served to show to the best possible advantage the Italo-American design-name which she displayed in her windows. She was not aware that her assistants were making use of items from this sort of trousseau which she'd entrusted to them, combined with other articles picked up from Josselyne's at the flea market and new stocks from the fifties. France, who came from Martinique, was always acting the Hollywood heroine from bush, jungle and tropics, revised and improved on to suit her whims as a half-caste trying to charm Paris, while spitting with disgust, Rasta fashion, on *Babylon* – the corrupting, moribund West of the Whites.

Zingha

Anyway, France had recently been calling herself *Zingha*, after the celebrated seventeenth-century Queen of Angola, who had dazzled and terrified the Portuguese colonizers up to the time of her death. Fascinating and fearless, she had been a warrior chief for nearly half a century, respected by her soldiers and her enemies. Every time France was asked 'Zingha? Why Zingha?' she told the story of this queen, who the White people had never heard of. On the other hand, she never said anything about herself. Her mother, a single parent bringing up seven children at La Redoute, near Fort-de-France, had sent her to France with a bursary, to live with an aunt who was supposed to see about sending her to school. But her schooling had been disrupted because her aunt, who worked as a nurse-aid in child welfare hospitals, had never managed to hold on to a single one of the fathers of her children. She had shacked up with several, but after the second child the father would leave her without any allowance. She had five children to bring up and France had acted as maid-of-all-work up to the day she'd dared to protest; her aunt kept a young West-Indian who wouldn't work and loved smart cars and the latest hi-fi sets. France had had frequent quarrels with her aunt over this temporary lover who she called a gigolo. Eventually the aunt kicked the gigolo out when France told her he'd never stopped propositioning her ever since she arrived. Her aunt could have defended her lover and called her a slut and thrown her out. She believed France, who was telling the truth, but a few months later France realized that a new young man was replacing the former one and that her aunt couldn't make up her mind to live alone, with no man in the house, or rather in her bed, even temporarily. She told her this the day she decided to leave to go and live with Zouzou, sharing the rent for the room between them, working from time to time as shop-assistants, telephonists or dance hostesses, but never going on the game. Often members of the gang or people who knew them at work thought they were making out together. Once a pal had asked them if they slept in the same bed, they hadn't answered. France was really beautiful. If she hadn't sympathized with the ideas of the Women's Movement, she might have had no scruples about accepting proposals for model agencies, but she'd always said no, which Zouzou couldn't understand. They argued every time France told Zouzou about her refusals. 'I'm not just a pretty face . . . These folks get on my tits.' Zouzou tried to explain to her that it had nothing to do with prostitution. 'Oh yeah! . . . you think fashion photographers are all queer? I've got pals who've told me they had to sleep with them because of the competition . . . and you often find those girls ending up at the Katmandu, a women's club, picking up shags . . . they've told me so themselves. I'm not making anything up. I've no wish to land in that shit. It's not the fact that they go for women that upsets me, it's the reason why they do it. It reminds me of a call-girl, a dago like me, who can't stand blokes but loves the dough so much she'll never give it up. She's young and a good-looker. She dresses like Catherine Deneuve, real class, but she drinks and shoots up. She's had the most incredible affairs with women. She just needs to hurt someone. She's impossible. I met her at a party, where she got pissed on vodka and the woman who'd invited her, a writer or journalist who wanted her to give up her job and those rotten blokes, had to pick her up, like a man – fortunately the girl was tiny and slight – to carry her to her car . . . no, no, Zouzou. I don't want that sort of life. Better off dead.'

Zouzou and France were popular at parties,

131

with the men as much as the women. They were aware of this and protected themselves from envy and their own narcissism by surrounding themselves with the girls and blokes from their gang. They always wore earrings or brooches which attracted people in the fashion business, and unusual make-up, never too way-out, which drew little cries of admiration and delight from the circle that gravitated towards them.

When they arrived with Sherazade, the regulars didn't rush to exchange the ritual kisses. They watched them. The three of them had sat down on the silky cushions arranged around the central palm tree, a real palm tree with spreading green fronds, but no dates, which reached up to the balconies of a gallery which went all the way round inside the enormous square hall, like a Moorish courtyard, or rather salon. They laughed and rolled about on the round over-stuffed cushions on which it was impossible to sleep softly. They got up to dance. It was hard rock. France demanded some genuine reggae. Sherazade danced as well as France. Suddenly they were the only ones under the palm tree; the others were watching them, standing round them in a circle as compact as the rings round the African or Moroccan drummers on the fore-court outside Beaubourg ... Suddenly they looked like tourists or provincials wandering around in the heart of Paris ... One of them remarked on this and they all scattered and fled into the corners of the room or on to the empty balconies.

Gradually, they approached the three girls and sniffed around Sherazade. They didn't address her directly.

'What's your pal's name?'

'Sherazade.'

'What?'

'Sherazade.'

'You taking the piss?'

'No. Ask her.'

'Really?'

'Yes.'

'Hold me up, hold me up or I'll pass out . . . Is someone putting on an act or what . . . The Grand Vizier's daughter under a palm tree . . . I must be dreaming . . .'

'What's got into him?' asked Sherazade. 'Is he crazy or what. OK. I'm splitting. All these silly buggers get on my tits.'

The bloke who'd pretended to swoon at Sherazade's feet, under the palm tree, had rallied his whole little clan, artistic directors, fashion photographers, editors of women's magazines . . . A cinema producer, who preferred Nordic or Irish blondes, and as Zouzou, France and Sherazade were rather Eastern Mediterranean types, and even slightly Negroid . . . They crowded around Sherazade like groupies on a pop platform.

Sherazade snatched the camera from one

photographer she'd seen snooping after her for some time who had taken advantage of the momentary confusion to take a shot of her. She hurled the camera on the floor a few yards away and went off with Zouzou without taking any notice of the crisis she was provoking. The camera had cost a small fortune. Sherazade had thrown it down so violently that it had broken. The photograher was weeping with fury. 'The bitch, I'll make her pay for it, let me just catch her, I'll make her pay for it . . . That sort turns up where they don't belong, gives everyone the come-on, just a bunch of prick-teasers, showing off with their pals, both lezzies, and then smashes people's property into the bargain . . . I need that for my work . . . I'll make her pay for it.' France was still there. She hadn't heard the photographer's insults or the final thundering conclusion to his monologue, 'And the little sluts can go back to their own country.' His friends for the evening had abandoned him, fearing the crisis and its consequences. He found himself alone, his camera seriously damaged. It was three a.m.

Zouzou suggested that Sherazade sleep at their place. There was a foam mattress and a sleeping bag. Sherazade hesitated.

'Come on! Tomorrow's Sunday. You can sleep late. I'll go and get croissants for you and France; I know where you can get them near me, at the top of Rue Faubourg-Saint-Denis, it's not far, I can easily walk there.'

'You coming?'

'No. I'll wait for France with you, then I'll go.'

At that moment France arrived with the gang, a bit pissed and rather noisy. They recounted the scene with the camera and looked at Sherazade all admiration.

'Watch out!' said a boy with a crew-cut and black and white *chiné* jacket. 'That guy's real mean, I know him, I know where he spends his evenings, what clubs he hangs out in, I can tip you off . . . He wanted to take a shot of me with my bike, I refused, he wouldn't take no for an answer. He even offered to pay me, he works for a magazine like *Playboy* or *Lui*, he's got dough for his expenses. I still said no. Every time he sees me he says, "Listen Omar, I don't go in for porn. Just you on your bike, that's not porn after all. I've got this super red leather cat-suit you can keep, not just for the photo, if you want it we can talk . . . And then, you know, the photos aren't for a paper, no one'll see them if that's what's worrying you, it's for me personally, you understand." I said I quite understood. But he still tries it on, all honey, "Omar, listen . . ." Now I avoid him. OK. Who'll I give a lift to?'

Omar dropped Sherazade in the Horloge district about 3.30 a.m.

Sherazade

What Sherazade didn't know, because she still hadn't contacted Meriem, in spite of the letters she wrote regularly but never sent to Anna-Maria whose address she knew by heart, in spite of the messages she heard on Radio-Beurs, Radio-Sunshine and Radio-Tipsy, in spite of the ads bearing her name in *Libération* and *Sans Frontière*, was that a week after she ran away, her father had decided to report her disappearance at the nearest police station. The inspector told her father it was a bit late for their inquiries to lead to anything. Sherazade's father hadn't wanted to go to the police, on account of the family, the neighbourhood, the nasty rumours that always spread, the *disgrace*, this word repeated and going from mouth to mouth, thousands and thousands of times, for any action which went counter to the law of tradition, ever since the housing estate had been inhabited by North Africans. The inspectors knew that Arabs don't like having to deal with the French police, and avoided making complaints or reporting missing persons or even losses and thefts.

The father waited two days, then three, then put it off to the next day . . . On the eighth day he realized Sherazade had really disappeared, that she'd run away, of her own free will. The inspector who interviewed him made him fill up a form on which he read: Statement re missing person. He'd hesitated before beginning to write. It was a veritable data card about himself and his daughter. He hadn't known what to put in the space reserved for how she disappeared: *Circumstances under which the person in question went missing.* On the form he wrote: 'My daughter Sherazade did not come home after school.'

That was all he knew. His wife hadn't told him she'd noticed clothes were missing from the drawer with the red mark, clothes she was quite familiar with as she was the one who washed them and she'd even cut some of them out when she'd still had time for sewing, before the birth of her last two, the twin girls. She used to make clothes for the whole family, particularly for special occasions. She'd also hidden from her husband something she only discovered a few days later; Sherazade had taken the thick white woollen *burnous* that a cousin had sent from Algeria for the eldest boy who wouldn't ever wear it, and also her own jewellery. She didn't say anything to anyone and never showed in public or even in the family how upset she was.

The father had also had to fill in the *description* on the back. He'd been obliged to stop several times to ask the inspector for explanations. For example, he didn't know what to put for *Race/ Colour*; and he rang his wife to ask about distinguishing marks also asking her for details for where it said *description*, garments, underclothes, shoes, hairstyle, jewellery, sundries, and also for *accessories and any peculiarities*. The inspector was growing impatient. It was taking a long time. The father didn't want to write just anything. It lasted an hour and Sherazade's father had left blanks in the description. The inspector put explicit questions to him and filled them in himself. For *lips* he asked, 'thin or fleshy?' He put 'fleshy' because the father said they weren't thin. For *hair colour: dyed/natural* the inspector said, 'Is your daughter a natural blonde, red-head or brunette?' He put down 'natural' after the father replied, 'She's got black hair', and for *length of hair* he noted 'pony-tail' after the father's laborious description, as he couldn't find the right words for his daughter's hairstyle. Before he signed the form the inspector said it was absolutely essential to have a photograph for identification. Under the heading *underclothes*, the father didn't dare write bra and the inspector didn't ask for details about

this; he passed the statement to Sherazade's
father.

NOTIFICATION

Description of missing person:

Race/Colour:
  North African

Apparent age: 17 years

Face:
  complexion: sallow
  shape: round
  forehead: high
  eyes: green
  nose: straight
  lips: fleshy
  chin: round

Height: 1.65m

Build: 48kg

Hair:
  colour: black
  type: curly
  length: long
  dyed/natural:
    natural
  style: pony-tail

Beard:

Moustache:

Marks/Scars/Visible:
  Small scar on left of chin

Description

a) clothes worn by missing person
(underclothes, outer garments, shoes, head-
dress, jewellery, sundries):
  panties: red
  slacks: green corduroy
  blouse: plaid
  pullover: navy blue
  jacket: navy blue
  footwear: brown boots
  head-dress: plastic slide

jewellery: gold earrings
sundries: shoulder bag
b) accessories and any peculiarities:
green plastic satchel
Information regarding place of work and other
places regularly visited by missing person:
school
Municipal Library

The form had been duly completed and signed. The father would bring the identity photo of his daughter the next day. The inspector informed the father that a telegram would be sent to the Paris Metropolitan Police and the police of the three Departments, and a telex would be sent to the Youth and Community Sections of the police. In case of urgency – if suicide were suspected – there would be a national broadcast to all police headquarters, and airport and border police would be notified.

Although he was discreet, Sherazade's father hadn't thought the police would make inquiries after a week. In his absence, his wife had to deal with inspectors who called and asked her to answer questions. She pretended to have difficulty in understanding French and the inspectors had to be satisfied with curt replies. The mother couldn't stop them searching the wardrobe in which she pointed out Sherazade's drawer. They had the discretion – because she was present? – not to search the other drawers or the hanging part and the shelves. They asked her where her daughter's bedroom was. She showed them the room with three beds, two of which were bunks, a table and the writing desk where she worked. They looked at the school books – Sherazade had taken her private notebooks – and a small Larousse dictionary.

'Did your daughter get any mail?'

'No.'

'No letters? Nothing?'

'No.'

'Has she written since she left?'

'No.'

'Have you anything else you can tell us?'

'No.'

The inspectors left the house without any clues, without getting on the track of anything interesting. They had been polite. The mother told no one she'd found a note that she'd got Meriem to read – 'Mum, I'm leaving tomorrow. Don't worry. Your daughter, Sherazade.' She told Meriem and Sherazade's father she'd found a road map of Algeria under her daughter's mattress.

The inspectors visited the school and then the Municipal Library. They'd never had occasion to go there, they were from the neighbourhood but at their age they preferred the football field to the library. They found it vast and light, pleasant. They noticed the newspapers, dailies

141

and magazines that they glanced at while waiting for the head librarian. They saw a young
woman in jeans approaching, which surprised
them: a librarian ought to wear a pleated skirt
and flat walking shoes. She had on a very bright
Jacquard pullover in reds, yellows, greens. The
inspectors walked over to her, introduced themselves and spoke of Sherazade. The young
woman didn't seem surprised and the inspectors, or rather one of them, the most observant,
wondered for a moment if this progressive
young woman might not possibly be harbouring
the missing girl. He didn't give any indication of
his suspicions, but promised himself to get hold
of the librarian's home address and to have her
discreetly shadowed. She spoke enthusiastically
about Sherazade, told them she read a lot, particularly the North African writers, she mentioned
Feraoun, Dib, Boudjedra, Djebar, Farès, Haddad,
Yacine, Roblès, Memmi, Choukri, Ben Jelloun,
Moroccan poets . . . but as they didn't appear to
have heard of them she interrupted her list and
showed them several shelves that they glanced
at distantly. 'It's thanks to Sherazade and other
schoolgirls like her that I have these shelves on
North Africa . . . they aren't reserved, more and
more readers from Aulnay, French people, bor-
row books that it wouldn't have occurred to
them to ask for before.' The inspectors weren't
interested in the problem of readers, they didn't
take many notes. They got the librarian to tell

them the exact times and days the missing girl spent at the library 'nearly every day for an hour at least', but she couldn't say the exact time of day.

The next day, the father came back to the police station with an identity photo his wife had discovered in a little drawer where she kept the children's photos. One Saturday afternoon, she was shopping for the family with Sherazade. At a certain moment her daughter had disappeared with a laugh behind the pleated curtain of a Photomaton booth. She'd suggested her mother sit next to her on the little revolving stool, but her mother refused. She'd kept the strip of photos of Sherazade which showed her laughing heartily. The inspector took the picture, looked at it for a moment.

'She doesn't look unhappy, your daughter, have you seen?'

The father reached for the identity photo, he hadn't really looked at it. When his wife handed it to him, he'd noticed his daughter's hearty laugh and he'd thought of Sherazade with less resentment, even with a certain affection – he loved his daughter, in spite of everything, and she did not know it. He suddenly felt very unhappy and his hands trembled slightly when he gave the Photomaton picture back to the inspector. The inspector was in a hurry, he didn't notice anything.

'We'll keep you informed, don't worry.'

143

Algeria

After the Tropical and Palm Tree evening with
Zouzou and France, Omar had given Sherazade
a lift back to the Horloge district. She jumped off
the bike and walked up to Julien's flat. She rang
several times. Julien opened the door. She'd not
seen him wearing that light cotton kimono, with
little black and white checks before. She said,
'I'm going to have a bath, will you lend it me?'

She shut herself in the bathroom with the
radio. She sang as she soaped herself. She always began with her feet, and as she meticulously scrubbed her toes, one after the other,
from the littlest to the biggest, starting with the
right foot always the right before the left, she'd
no idea why, she simultaneously saw in her
mind's eye the solitary Arab who she sometimes
met in the neighbourhood, with his blanket
folded over his shoulder like a carpet seller and
his bottle of Evian water in his hand. He was a

vagabond who slept rough under the bridges of the overground Metro. He talked to himself in French with an Arab accent and never spoke to anyone. One morning she'd seen him sitting on a sort of crate, barefoot, with his trousers rolled up to his calves. He was washing his feet, just like her grandfather did, but using the Evian water, under the bridge, near a Metro station. He put the clean foot down on a piece of cardboard in front of the crate. He'd started with the right foot, absorbed in his toilet as if he were in the sandy courtyard of an Algerian village house, in fine weather. This man, astray in the city, washing his feet, reminded her of her grandfather, preparing to say his prayers. He didn't know that she and Meriem, sitting under the fig-tree, where they were dressing their dolls made out of two olive twigs fixed together in a cross then covered with strips of cloth for the body, always watched him performing his ablutions and followed his movements until he prostrated himself on his prayer mat. He had taught them the words but not the ablutions. They sometimes amused themselves, when he was not there, washing like him, first their faces and heads several times, their arms up to the elbow, their feet up to the ankles. They argued when one of them corrected the other over the way she did a foot or her face. The next few times, they watched the grandfather carefully and pointed out in a whisper a detail that had escaped them.

145

One day the grandfather had scolded Sherazade for playing with the *tayemoum*, the smooth stone he kept near his prayer mat to use for his ablutions. In the mosques and homes, one always saw one of these smooth stones near the prayer mats, that Sherazade thought just right for playing hopscotch under the fig-trees. The grandfather had had to explain to Sherazade and Meriem, standing in front of him, that he needed the *tayemoum* for his ablutions when he prayed about four o'clock in the morning when water was scarce: you smoothed your hand over the stone then over the parts of your body you had to wash, as if the stone had been water. He showed them how he did it. From that day, Sherazade respected her grandfather's *tayemoum*.

Sherazade looked round but couldn't see a pumice stone for her heels.

She slipped on the check kimono and dried her feet as the floor near the bath was wet.

The shutters were down in the two rooms. Sherazade crept into Julien's bed, on his right. He wasn't asleep.

146

Kwakker

Sherazade didn't see anyone at the squat when she got back. Had they all left in a few days? The kitchen was still in the usual shambles, the fridge empty and dirty, crockery heaped up in the sink and on the draining-board. She didn't find any letters for her on her bed. There was nothing lying about; she realized Djamila had gone. In Pierrot's and Basile's bedroom, everything was in the same state. The beds unmade, tables cluttered up, books lying open next to the bedside lamps, piled up among newspapers. Sherazade took two letters for Pierrot out of the inside pocket of her blouson and put them on his bed, near the pillow. She glanced at the latest copy of *Libé*, it was three days old. She knew where the .38s were kept. They were not there. Had they done a hold-up, an act of terrorism? She'd have heard if it had gone wrong. The papers, the radio would have mentioned it.

She'd seen nothing, heard nothing. As they never left compromising papers at the squat, knowing the police could arrive at any moment, on the pretext of looking for drugs, or with no excuse, Sherazade could find nothing to give her a clue.

Someone was coming, it was Krim. He greeted her in Arabic, she replied in French.

'You've decided to be a *harki* today? What's up with you? You speak Arabic, don't you?'

'Yes. But I don't feel like speaking Arabic today, that's all.'

'What's got into you?'

'Everyone's cleared off and you never let me know. You don't tell me anything.'

'Who knew where you were?'

'No one.'

'Well then. Pierrot's coming back tomorrow; he's gone to Germany; he spent three days with his folks in the North. Don't ask why he's gone to Germany ... You can be sure it's not for the pacifists ... anyway, I've no idea. You know Pierrot ... I play music with him, he's good, for the rest ...'

'And Basile?'

'Pierrot wanted Basile to go with him. Basile said he could shift for himself, he speaks German. Pierrot didn't insist. I've got the impression they're preparing a job in his group, always busy, always secret ... Anyway, I don't ask any questions. They plot things with Basile. I hear them sometimes in the night. Besides, you know Pierrot was going crazy, looking for you everywhere . . . In the end he thought of suicide. Basile said "You'd like that, that'd settle everything." They quarrelled. Every day he asked if you'd been back, if anyone'd seen you. Once Basile told him, "I've seen her in a bar in Pigalle, she was soliciting." You should have seen Pierrot . . . he started to yell. "It's not true, you're lying, you say that to screw me up, it wasn't her, and if it's true and I catch her, I'll do the blokes in . . . I'll do them . . ." Basile cut him short and said, "What about her? What'll you do to her?" Pierrot said, "Nothing. I won't do anything to her." In the end, Basile told him it wasn't true, he didn't know where you kip down when you're not at the squat, you're free to come and go where you please. Pierrot said, "Sure," but he went on looking for you until he left for the North. Basile's made quite a pile working for house-movers and he's gone to Africa. He said he was going to look for a wife there, a real one, a Negress, not a rotten *Babylon* woman, a black woman from the bush and he wasn't ever coming back here or going back to Guadeloupe . . .'

'You believe him?'

'No. But it's true he's in Africa. He sent a letter to Pierrot from the Ivory Coast.'

'When's he coming back?'

'Nobody knows. If you want to know the lot, Driss is in prison. He got nicked by the police with a syringe on him and some smack. He must have been blown that evening, or else he was asking for it, I dunno. He's in Fleury-Merogis* if you want to see him or write to him.'

'I'll write to him. Give me the address.'

'You see, I'm really about the only one here. Djamila's gone to Algeria. She's been wanting to go for a long time, a complicated family story. I couldn't follow what Eddy told me; he was rather upset that day, the day he got here and she'd left already, when she'd promised him, sworn they'd both go to Tunisia first. He'd started making all the arrangements, the journey, the plane tickets, a car when they arrived . . . he comes back in the evening, very pleased, he calls me, he calls Pierrot everyone, "I'm going to Tunisia, I'm going to Tunisia . . .", we say, "OK, that's no big deal", and he says, "Yes it is, it's the first time, I was scared before." I asked him, "What about the sax? We need you for rehearsals." He said for the time being he couldn't give a fuck, in any case he'd be back and he just wanted to see Djamila to explain everything to her. We told him Djamila must be in Algeria already. "I'm going to look for her . . . I'll get the tickets changed I'll go straight to Algeria." I thought it's no joke being in love

* Prison situated to the south of Paris. There is a shuttle bus service from Denfert-Rochereau to take families who wish to visit prisoners. (Trans.)

with birds who do a bunk, 'cos blokes have to spend their time running after them. Look at you, Pierrot always wants to know where you are and Eddy's catching the plane this evening for Algiers . . . they must be mad or sick . . . And you think he'll find her, Djamila?'

'Yes, I think so . . . well, if she wants him to. Does he know she's in Setif?'

'I think so. But I'm in the shit with these musicians who bugger off . . . Now there's no one but me. I'll have to find another group, it's no joke guys like that, I ought to've had my suspicions of these militants living in the past and guys in love it's no go. If you're into music you give up everything else, you got to be a fanatic like an ayatollah . . . Can you sing?'

'I like singing.'

'Want to try?'

'OK, but first you teach me to ride the bike, you promised.'

'That's true. Come on then.'

Krim spent all evening teaching Sherazade to ride his Kwakker. He'd not hesitated to let her have a try on his favourite bike. He felt she'd have the knack and it wouldn't be hard to get her to learn quickly. At the end of the lesson, Sherazade said to Krim, 'Will you find me one like this?'

'For you, yes. I'm sure you won't wreck it. But give me time.'

Very soon, Sherazade could ride Krim's bike

151

by herself. She borrowed his leathers, they were a bit big for her although Krim was fairly thin and not very tall. One day, she rode by herself all the way to Etampes. When she told Krim, he gave her a rocket, she could have got herself stopped by the cops, she was a juvenile, without a licence . . . she'd have gone to join Driss, but in the women's prison. Sherazade said she wouldn't have stopped, she'd have put a spurt on and shaken them off. 'Sure, sure . . .' Krim replied.

Vero

'You know,' Krim said to Sherazade, after the
first bike session, 'there's some new people at
the squat, you didn't see them as they were
sleeping; they're in Driss and Eddy's room. They
get grants from the DASS and are on job training, him as a welder and boiler-maker, her as a
hairdresser. They're nineteen or twenty at the
most. She's always looking for someone to cut
their hair, for practice, but nobody wants her to,
not even Rachid who she's with at the moment.
Her name's Vero. Rachid laughs at her because
of her *pied-noir* accent. She's a scream, she takes
off her mother who had to leave Algeria after
independence. She comes from Oran, but she's
of Spanish origin. Vero says her mother doesn't
like Arabs. When she phoned her in Nice to tell
her she was going to marry Rachid, her mother
burst into tears. "What my girl, are you crazy, I
didn't bring you up till now to give you to an

Arab." Vero told her Rachid's a Kabyle, it's not the same thing, but her mother went on, "My poor girl you's completely mad, Arab – Kabyle, six of one half a dozen of the other, make's no odds, all the same filthy race, you can't possibly do that to me, your mother, you listen my girl." Vero wouldn't listen and said she was putting Rachid on the line and the mother was obliged to say hello politely. Rachid talked nicely to Vero's mother who said, "You sure you're an Arab? You talk like a Frenchman from Paris." Rachid explained he was born in Paris, but his parents are Kabyles. The mother, when she spoke to Vero again, repeated, "My girl, he's an Arab, he said so himself, your poor mother's so wretched." Vero told her if she refused to receive Rachid in her house, she'd never see her, Vero, Véronique, her own daughter again.'

Vero made them all laugh with her comic turns. She was small, a real little dumpling; she dressed in mini-skirts that barely covered her fat thighs when she sat down. She wore black stockings, socks coming half-way up her calves and ballet-slippers. She put on a lot of make-up and was always wanting to kiss Rachid who said, "No, you've got lipstick on today," as she couldn't exist without make-up you wondered when Rachid could kiss her. She had a big mouth, with bright red lipstick and laughed all the time. She had huge sleepy eyes, outlined in black and drawn up towards her temples. You

154

could see her skin was white and smooth under the rouge that she rubbed off without noticing when she waved her hands over her face. Exuberant and jolly, she was also very noisy. After what Krim told her, Sherazade wondered if she would get on with Vero.

That night, Sherazade slept at the squat.

Julien

Julien was waiting for Sherazade. She didn't phone and he knew she hung up if the answer-phone was switched on. A chance remark about these shitty machines. Julien realized she was the person who refused to speak after the bleep . . .

Since she'd been working, Sherazade didn't come to the library. Julien went on with his research, but not so intently. He'd begun to write a scenario that he'd mentioned to a film-director friend. Julien told him he'd show him photos of the girl he was thinking about for the heroine of the film. Sherazade often spent Sundays with Julien. She read the books she hadn't had time to read during the week and that she took down from Julien's shelves, the ones he bought thinking they might interest Sherazade. She never asked him for any, but he thought of them for her. She talked to him more about what she'd just read than about herself. He didn't even know where she worked or what she did. He'd asked her one morning as she was getting ready in the bathroom. She'd answered, with her mouth full of toothpaste, 'In a fashion boutique with Zouzou and France.' When he asked for more details, she didn't answer.

On Sunday mornings, if she'd slept at Julien's, Sherazade went to buy a fresh baguette and brought him a glass of orange juice while he was still dozing. She would shake him affectionately and put the glass down on the carpet. Julien would get up, saying, 'You've already got your walkman over your ears. So early. Not yet dressed . . . It's a bad habit . . . and I can't even put on some opera.'

He would go and have a bath. Often, Sherazade who kept the black and white kimono on all morning, would join him in the bathroom, sitting on the edge of the bath or the bidet, and they'd chat.

Julien would stretch out in the water.

Sometimes they spoke Arabic, since Sherazade had noticed books written in Arabic script on the work-table and Julien had told her he knew this language; they laughed at each other's accents and sometimes recorded their talk to listen to each other and laugh at their blunders. Julien taught Sherazade words of literary Arabic and Sherazade made him repeat after her expressions in the Algerian dialect she spoke with her mother and that her grandfather had begun to teach her to read and write in Algeria, with her sister Meriem. The two girls used to sit side by side, holding a slate; the grandfather gave them a lesson every day. But they hadn't stayed long enough in their mother's home village. In France, they'd soon forgotten what their grandfather had taught them.

Sherazade told Julien popular Algerian stories which he didn't know. He laughed with her over the bizarre adventures of Djeha. She also talked to him about things to do with the Algerian War that their grandfather had liked to tell his two grandchildren, who'd been brought up in France and might not have heard about there . . . as if nothing had happened, as if they hadn't gained anything, those Algerians who today and for some years now were emigrating to the land of mirages, as they called France. They were becoming Roumiettes, little Europeans, were Meriem and Sherazade, his favourites who were going back to the foreign country, living among infidels. Their grandfather spent long hours with them in the courtyard of the house, in the fields where they accompanied him. They listened to him, from time to time opening their mouths for a ripe fig which he selected, not too big, one for each. He spoke to them of Allah, simply. He told them legends and said, 'Your grandmother would have told you even finer stories if she'd been alive, but she died during the war.' The girls asked him about their grand-mother's death but he wouldn't answer. They'd insisted and he'd said, 'Don't talk any more about that.'

Julien was happy.

And then suddenly, Sherazade brought the conversation to an abrupt end with 'I'm going biking this afternoon.'

'All alone?'

'No. With Krim.'

'Who's he?'

'A buddy.'

'You coming back?'

Sherazade didn't reply, got dressed after a rapid toilet and left.

Julien hadn't the energy to get out of the bath, or to add hot water. The phone rang, forcing him to get out of the cold water, which was still clean as he hadn't washed. He knew it wasn't Sher-azade. He was disappointed because it wasn't her. If he hadn't got photographs he needed to print, he'd accept Enrico's suggestion to go to a committee meeting for the magazine, *Combat for the Diaspora*.

When he got home, he finished working on a game programme for the computor.

On Sundays, if Sherazade didn't go off sud-denly, without leaving any way of getting in touch with her – and he thought he might never be able to see her again and he'd never see her again because he knew nothing about her.

159

Should he give her description to the police? He wouldn't go as far as that – Julien took photos. She let him do so but never obeyed his injunctions when he said, 'Raise your head, look at me, don't sit down . . .' In the evening, he'd find on his table up to six, ten reels, each of thirty-six poses. Every time he'd say to himself . . . 'I'm crazy, completely crazy.' He'd start again at the first opportunity. He'd spend the night developing and printing them; he'd start again if he wasn't completely satisfied.

Sherazade made no attempt to see the photos. He'd been the one to insist on showing them to her and she couldn't avoid seeing the ones he pinned up on his cork board and all over the flat.

He was there when she came back from the bike ride, flushed from the wind; he wanted to take some photos but he gave up the idea; he was afraid she'd go off immediately. She'd kept on Krim's leather cat-suit as he had several. Julien still hesitated, got up to fetch the camera but came back to Sherazade, empty-handed. He stroked her cheeks.

'Will you show me your bike?'

'It isn't mine.'

She took off the leathers. She was wearing a white T-shirt and red tights. She put on a pair of jeans and her blouson but took out of a bag clothes that Julien hadn't noticed, something looking like a sort of battle-dress.

'You going off?'

'I'm meeting Zouzou and France.'

He was about to say, 'Can I come?' but held his tongue, knowing she'd say, 'No.' If she'd wanted, she'd have suggested it but she never let him share her other life. She was about to leave with her bag and her clothes. He thought she might not come back.

'How d'you feel about watching a film?'

'Dunno, perhaps . . . anyway, I'm late. 'Bye!'

Julien hurried to the table in the bedroom on which Sherazade sometimes left a bag, a sort of holdall. He didn't spot it straight away. He couldn't stop trembling, he had a cramp in his stomach; fortunately he was alone, he felt weak and guilty at the same time. He rummaged in the bag. He saw several red and black Chinese notebooks which he didn't touch. He felt better, he'd managed not to be indiscreet. He just took out two Michelin maps, a road map of France and one of Algeria. He put them back . . . He'd not done anything serious, after all. He hadn't committed a crime.

He watched Godard's *A bout de souffle* once more.

Jungle

Sherazade met Zouzou and France at the Halles in a brasserie which was still deserted at that time. They needed to talk. They had to finalize a plan for the evening. Zouzou was Tunisian; petite and plump, with a copper-coloured complexion and a lively, childish face which made you immediately feel you wanted to talk to her, touch her, love her. Her real name was Zoulikha, but everyone called her Zouzou. People were afraid of France, they adored Zouzou. You always wondered how they could be together like this, nearly twenty-four hours out of twenty-four, and no one up till now had managed to separate them. Some men said, 'Just wait, they're young, it won't last', and when they met them at parties or dropped in to see them at the boutique, they continued to chat up Zouzou. France was beautiful and unapproachable, she frightened you off. You wondered what reason she had to be so stuck-up – after all, when you're a half-caste from Martinique, you're descended from slaves – in spite of these reassuring thoughts people remained apprehensive. You never saw her laugh except when she was with the boys and girls from the gangs they both hung out with. They often heard people say of them, 'They've got the most incredible *look*.' Zouzou had accepted a private invitation from a well-known fashion photographer. He'd told her he wanted all three of them, he'd have things for them to wear, but if they wanted to they could bring way-out clothes they were fond of. He'd spoken in a roundabout way of daring pictures which were nice little earners especially of three girls together – exotic beauties – . . . It'd be a lark for them and they'd earn a pile for doing more or less nothing . . . They just had to listen to him, do what he asked, he knew the punters' tastes – women as well as men – he added to prove the extent of the business, it was all private sales, the punters were very generous and you could rely on their discretion. Zouzou let him develop his arguments. She couldn't wait to tell France and Sherazade about it.

In their break at the fast-food, Zouzou told them the whole story, adding ,'I said yes.'

'What! you said yes without knowing if we'd agree? You going alone?' asked France who'd have no truck with this way of behaving . . .

She'd only pretended to be angry. They'd keep

the appointment, and they worked out a suitable collective countermeasure. Already, Zouzou could hardly control her laughter at the thought.

In the brasserie, Sherazade opened her bag; at the bottom, hidden under the battle-dress, were three pistols she'd bought in a toy shop, perfect replicas of the real thing. She took them out, 'Just like .38s,' she told the girls who were very impressed. 'Those are the pistols used by the Italian Autonomes. Pierrot and Basile have got real ones.'

They took a taxi to an elegant building in the Seventh Arrondissement, near the Avenue Bosquet. Zouzou checked the address. She hadn't been given any name. She'd been told third floor, door on the left. Zouzou rang and the door was opened. The flat was opulent, but with very little furniture. Heavy red and gold velvet curtains everywhere, and Chinese screens. The photographer took them to one end of a vast empty room with cameras on tripods and powerful spots. Everything was set up. He pointed to a chest stuffed with clothes near one of the screens. 'Take what you like.' While France and Sherazade were dressing up, whispering together behind the first screen, Zouzou took the photographer on one side and got him to advance the money: a thousand francs each. 'But see you do exactly what I say.' 'Yes' said Zouzou with her most captivating smile, 'Of course' – 'Right, let's go!' said the photographer patting her on the behind. 'To work.' France and Sherazade were ready. France was a tigress in yellow and black regular striped mini-skirt; Sherazade a zebra in irregular black and white striped hot-pants; both wore black fishnet stockings and off-the-shoulder tops. Their hair was teased to look like a mane and they each had a wide barbarian's belt such as Spartacus was supposed to have worn. Zouzou put on a leopard outfit consisting of split shorts and a top that barely covered her breasts. She had on red stockings that the photographer asked her to take off 'I prefer bare legs.' Her belt allowed her, like France and Sherazade, to hide her pistol.

He looked them over.

He approached them and with a professional touch bared a breast here, a buttock there, and pulled Sherazade's *décolleté* a bit lower. 'You're fantastic. Jungle and virgin forest scenes are very popular at the moment . . . We ought to have a panther as well, but I've got a suitable outfit in the chest. We'll have that later. Wait, I've got an idea, each of you take a sub-machine-gun, like guerrillas, I've got some there, real ones, unloaded. Toy guns are no use, these are better, you're not scared I hope, don't worry; look, I'll show you, there's no risk, they're not loaded; I don't want any blood and if I did for other scenes, I've got some haemoglobin or tomato ketchup, that always does the trick if you can't

165

stand the sight of blood. OK, let's start, you're
not shocked darlings I hope, Oh! you don't look
the goody-goody type I personally haven't much
time for them and their airs and graces, but you
three . . . You wouldn't have come. It's going to
be fabulous. Well this is what you do, first you
kiss on the lips you can pretend as soon as I say
"Now" you change partners as if you were
dancing in a nightclub – there really are discos
just for women – and then you lie down one on
top of the other in turn, it's quite simple. But see
that your tits and bums are visible, you mustn't
be prudish. If you were in a sauna or a Turkish
bath since that's the thing now, you'd be star-
kers and it wouldn't worry you, well now it's the
same thing. Let's start. You're wonderful the
photos'll be t'riff, brill, scoops . . . No it's not for
a newspaper, I work privately for this kind of
photo don't worry. Right, you ready? What are
you waiting for? The spots have been on all this
time, they'll burn out, they're expensive and
you've got to work fast . . . You ready? We're
starting. Come on Zouzou . . . You think you're
stars or something? You're not stars yet, are you!
and anyway in this business there aren't any
stars, so don't waste your time imagining you've
got there. OK, you've got nice bums, nice tits,
you're young, but there are thousands like you
queuing up for the job if you don't want it, no
problem for me . . . but I've already paid you; the
little one there's got the money, it's not cheap for

shags you can pick up anywhere, well come on, I'm not joking. Well, shit, can we start?'

They were standing in front of him, holding their pistols.

'Oh, ho! You don't mess about with me. What game d'you think you're playing? Where d'you think you are?'

'It's not a game. These are .38s. You know what those are? The Red Brigade who go in for knee-capping, you know about that? We're going to knee-cap you . . .' said Sherazade, still disguised as a veritable tigress; she continued, 'One of the three is loaded. It's like Russian Roulette you know what that is? We're going to screw up the whole show and scram. If you shoot your mouth off we'll bring a charge against you for inciting to prostitution, unmistakable case of procuring . . . We've got proof. You're well known. Besides, I'm wondering if we shouldn't just shoot you like a dog.'

The well-known photographer took his girl-guerrillas seriously and wasn't very happy. He didn't believe they'd shoot. He was right.

At the parties they subsequently attended there was no more talk of this well-known photographer, but a similar story to theirs circulated. There was no mention of a revolver. The girls in question had stopped a porn-merchant in his tracks with an anti-rape device and had beaten him up.

Godard

Julien was now watching *Pierrot le fou*. Sherazade arrived just when the car was going up in flames.

'That film again?'

'It's for my work. I'm watching how it's made. I can stop it when I like, and re-start ... it's brilliant, a video. Eustache worked with one, he had heaps of plans when he committed suicide.'

'Who's Eustache?'

'A French film director, who died for France.'

'Don't talk bullshit.'

'It's not bullshit. He wanted French cinema to be real cinema again, not crap, and he died for it. OK, I'm stopping, it's late. I'm working tomorrow.'

'Me too. Tonight I'll sleep in the single bed, I must get up early tomorrow.'

Julien didn't reply. Perhaps she'd join him in his bed as she sometimes did when she decided to sleep in the single bed where she'd spent the first night. Sherazade took off her blouson, took the banknotes out of the inside pocket, ten one-hundred-franc notes, and threw them on the table.

'That your wages?'

'One evening's wages, look, a thousand francs . . .'

'You on the game now? You turning tricks or what?'

'No, no! Don't get in a stew I'm going to tell you about it.'

For the first time, Sherazade told Julien a bit about her life elsewhere. Anxious at first, he burst out laughing with her as she acted the scene of the screwed-up photo session and the celebrated photographer's panic. She showed him the pistol that didn't look like a toy. When she'd finished telling him the story Sherazade said to Julien, 'You see what you can expect if you go on taking photos.'

'But I don't do porn.'

'It's the same thing . . . Anyway, just wait and see . . .'

She tore down all the pictures of herself that Julien had stuck or pinned everywhere from the kitchen to the bathroom, through the panelled walls of the bedroom and the big living-room, photos of every shape and size, from passport to poster. 'I'm sick to death of seeing my mug everywhere, you understand . . . you don't need me in the flesh after all . . .'

Julien, who wasn't used to scenes and still less to Sherazade's who never made any, stared at her in bewilderment.

'That's what I do with your play-acting.'

Sherazade meticulously tore up all the photos, one by one, from the smallest to the largest. She filled the waste-paper basket which she went to empty in the rubbish chute and started again. The photographic paper was best quality, thick and hard to cut. Sherazade continued till the very last pictures.

'I know you've got others in yellow Kodak boxes and in files, I'll leave you those. I'm tearing up the ones I don't want to see on the walls any more, that's all.'

Julien had not made the slightest move to stop her destroying these photos of which he had taken print after print till they were perfect. He'd shown some to his friend for the film-script, but he'd kept some that he greatly prized. Sherazade had destroyed them. He knew that if he'd wanted to stop her it would have led to a fight. In her fury he might have hurt her and he'd never have seen her again. So he'd watched her and finally, when the last scraps of his pictures were in the waste-paper basket, he felt that Sherazade was right. He wasn't angry with her.

He thought again about the scene she had described to him.

'Will you lend me your jungle scene?'

'What for?'

'For the film-script.'

'If you like. Are you making the film?'

'With you, yes. I'm finishing off the dialogue.
It's going to be fine. Will you read the script?'

'OK. And the chap who's making the film,
who's he?'

'A film-director pal, you don't know him. If
you like, we'll go and see him.'

'What's the story all about?'

'I'd rather not talk about it. Read it.'

Sherazade read Julien's script in the bath.
Julien came in to shave. He could see her in the
mirror above the basin.

'You've finished?'

'Yes.'

'Well, d'you like it?'

'Yes, but I think . . .'

Sherazade made some observations which
Julien listened to, blaming his tension on the
shitty razor, which didn't cut properly and was
the only one he'd got . . . He thought she could
be right and he'd change the script taking into
account what she'd said.

'It's very late, you know? I don't know about
you, but I'm going to bed, I've got work to do
tomorrow.'

'Me too . . . You're not the only one.'

'OK. 'Night!'

''Night!'

Julien waited a bit for Sherazade but fell

asleep just when she was getting into the single bed after winding up the alarm. It was three a.m.

Rachid

Pierrot was back from Germany. He was waiting
for Basile who would be coming via Italy on his
way back from Africa, after getting as far as
Tunisia. He hadn't heard from him and was
getting impatient.

The letters he'd sent Sherazade had arrived
the day before. Krim had put them on the table
in her room where she was sure to see them.
Pierrot had read Sherazade's two letters. Without knowing the reason he was in such a bad
mood, Krim had told him off and suggested a bit
of music. They'd shut themselves in the end
room. Krim had told Pierrot he'd do better
playing music instead of playing militants in
phony groups. Pierrot was very good on the
bass; he didn't feel like arguing.

There was a knock on the door. It was Basile.
He was wearing a new hat, 'guaranteed pure
bush', he said. Basile hugged Pierrot, then Krim,

Eastern fashion; he picked up his bag and distributed 'local gadgets'. Sherazade turned up just as Basile was taking a necklace for her out of his bag.

'A diamond necklace for Sherazade. Real diamonds, no Bokassa stuff.'

Basile got up, put his arms round Sherazade and turned her round three times before fastening the necklace round her neck.

'Queen Zingha,' he said.

'You've heard of her?' said Sherazade.

'Yes, why?'

'I've got a pal who calls herself Zingha.'

'A Negress?'

'Half Negress. She's from Martinique.'

'Oh, my!' said Basile. 'Where's your Zingha? I'd like to meet her. Is she pretty?'

'Prettier than Lisette Malidor . . .'

Krim asked Basile why he'd come back alone, without any bush Negress to protect him against *Babylon* where he was never going to set foot again. Basile made a vague gesture indicating don't let's talk about that and all three began playing. Krim told Sherazade to sing. Sherazade improvised. She had a good voice and the squatmates promised to engage her for their next gig.

'Meanwhile,' said Pierrot, 'you ought to take singing lessons.'

'Where?'

'At classes run by the municipality. They're free.'

174

Rachid opened the door and came into the middle of the room. He was alone, Vero was practising her hairdressing; he'd overslept that morning and intended to bunk off his boiler-making, he was sick of it . . . People were always making rude remarks to him, his tattoos, clothes, hair. They could all go to hell.

'Right, you Beurs, shall we do a take-off of *Carte de séjour*? You need an Arab singer. I can sing; I don't know much Arabic, I'm a Kabyle, but I can do a mixture . . . That'll satisfy everyone. Shall we try?'

Rachid sang, taking off sixties rock-singers. There was nothing he didn't know about rock, all the English, American, French groups. He'd been a member of gangs of young hoodlums, dressing successively as rocker, teddy-boy, weatherman; he'd kept all the outfits that he took with him everywhere in spite of Vero's reproaches that all that was out of fashion, old hat, and only fit to be chucked in the dustbin: his Mexican boots, leather jackets, denim waistcoat, genuine denim jeans, German boots, ranger's hats, scarves and belts, and especially his mohican that Vero always wanted to cut off because she thought it really common. But he was still keen on it and now he was the one who occupied the bathroom as long as Driss, with his gels and brilliantines for his mohican, that Vero threatened to throw away. Rachid had known gangs he'd never belonged to – Hell's Angels –

in the suburbs of Crimée, Créteil. He often bumped into them, but he didn't like their skinheads and the SS badges they flaunted. He'd had a Jewish girlfriend who'd reproached him for his interest in gangs which adopted Nazi badges, even if, as some of them claimed, it was just for a joke. He'd taken notice of what she'd said. She often talked about what happened to the Jews and about Hitler, he'd seen it on the telly, *Holocaust* it was called. She told him some members of her family had never returned from the camps. He thought of the Algerian War that he knew nothing about as nobody had ever talked to him about it, neither his father, nor his mother, nor the foster families he'd been put with, nor the social workers, nor the staff at the various homes he'd been in. His Jewish girl-friend had left him as she was sick of being dragged into his gangs of rockers where they never talked of anything but gear, shops where you could buy badges, rock groups she knew all that by heart: Gene Vincent, Eddie Cochran, everlasting Elvis, Matchbox, Crazy Cavan, Chuck Berry, Stray Cats . . . Rockabilly fans, rock 'n'roll fans who talked about revolt and violence but who were more worried about the lacquer for their hair and things they needed for their gear. She'd written to him quite nicely, explaining she wanted to look around a bit. He'd not seen her again. With Vero, it was easy. She didn't agonize so much.

Rachid couldn't sing, but he was very good at taking off all the stars the big names and the less well-known ones he knew indirectly through cassettes which he learnt by heart, copying their clothes, remembering everything he read about their private lives with the same enthusiasm his sisters showed in reading *Nous deux*.* Rachid read everything about his idols and his gang shared out among themselves everything they could find about the groups and the singers they liked. They had the insatiable appetite and obsession of all collectors.

'You ought to get taken on in a café-theatre,' Basile said to Rachid.

'What's that? I only know about gigs . . .'

'They're little theatres where they put on sketches, impersonations.'

'You two,' said Sherazade to Pierrot and Basile, 'you always know what's good for other people. And what about yourselves?'

'That's our business,' said Pierrot, getting up to leave with Basile.

* A women's magazine specializing in sentimental photo romances. (Trans.)

Pierrot

Nobody had thought to cover up Eddy's letter to Djamila, written with a thick felt-tip or a spraycan on the wall facing the mirror of the big room with the red armchair. Had Djamila read it before leaving for Algeria? It was a love-letter that everyone who came back to the squat had read as if it had been a letter addressed to them. They didn't know the letter had been written for Djamila, but those who knew Eddy guessed immediately. Eddy wrote poems that he sometimes read to the squat-mates when they were all together, but that was not often. He also wrote lyrics, 'specially' for their group he said. They were more interested in these than the poems. He typed out the songs, photocopied them and they worked on them together to improve them.

'It's more fun than your leaflets, Pierrot,' Basile said.

'They're not *my* leaflets . . .' Pierrot yelled,

178

'and what's more you get on my bloody nerves
the lot of you with your stupid little affairs with
petit-bourgeois dagos . . . you don't give a fuck
for what's happening all over the world even in
France . . . You don't give a fuck for the political
prisoners in Morocco in Latin America in Russia
in Africa in Europe in France as well and you
don't care a damn about torture . . . you're a
lousy self-satisfied bunch all you worry about is
your little gadgets and your dough . . . more and
more dough on the back of the Third World and
all the exploited peoples but you you're like little
old folk pensioners my comfort . . . my Mexican
boots my hi-fi my bike or my BMW to pick up a
bit of skirt my Saturday night gig champagne in
discos lying in deckchairs with a glass of lemon-
ade or Coca-Cola that all the future you think
about you've got nothing in your heads it's
incredible living it up letting your hair down
what's that mean that means touching fat pom-
pous loaded old gits for a hand-out swindling
them to do what after that to live like bourgeois
that's all you lot are after smart cars smart chicks
smart shoes and all the rest and not do a stroke
all pimps jerks living off women who sell their
ass so they can buy more rings more cars at ten
grand and blow all the dough they've earned
slaving away in stinking bars I want it all and I
want it now that's all you say and I say shit I
wonder why anyone gives a fuck you've forgotten all the Kaders bumped off by yellow-bellied

179

little Frenchmen scared shitless by cops filthy swine Kader in Vitry Zanouda in Vaulx-en-Vexin Laouri and Zahir in Marseilles and the suicides Djamel from Argenteuil Farid from Paris and all the ones we don't hear about you forget everything what use is your memory to you . . .'

Pierrot talked non-stop, beside himself with fury. Basile tried to calm him down but he didn't calm down; they all stood there flabbergasted, speechless, each on the point of leaving as it became intolerable. Never had they heard Pierrot talk like this. They knew he was impassioned, intelligent, sometimes carried away, but not so full of bitterness and hatred . . .

Sherazade fired a shot in the air with a warning pistol. They all began to speak and Pierrot fell silent. He was looking at Sherazade who realized that her letters had probably hurt him and was sorry she'd thought it necessary to write the truth. She said, 'Listen Pierrot . . .'

'Leave me alone, bugger off . . .'

Sherazade went over to him, put her arm round his shoulders and took him into her room. They sat down on Sherazade's red bedspread and she talked to him softly for a long time. Pierrot spoke too.

Pierrot told her he was soon leaving Paris for another town in France and Sherazade told him she wanted to leave for Algeria.

'If you like I'll take you, I'll have a car; I'm

going south-west.'

'You'll tell me when you're leaving?'

'But if you're not here . . .'

'I'll leave a phone number.'

Before she left, Sherazade went into the bathroom to brush her hair. On the glass shelf above the basin she saw three half-used strips of pills. Djamila was no longer there, she must have left some that nobody had thrown away, and Vero had piled up on the shelf all her beauty preparations and make-up with the pills as well. Sherazade shouted through the door, 'Rachid, tell Vero to put her pills somewhere else.'

'That's not my problem,' replied Rachid who couldn't give a damn about Vero's pills lying around or if she got mixed up with the doses . . . that was her problem.

Sherazade threw away the fag-ends which were accumulating on the edge of the basin and the shelf. They all smoked. She smoked occasionally, but not much.

Fromentin

When she left the squat Sherazade sat down on a bench in the boulevard near a phone box that had been occupied for a little time. She said to herself – if in one minute exactly, the call box is free, I'll ring Meriem. She suddenly felt a strong urge to hear her sister's voice and it had nearly made her feel like crying. The one minute passed, the man was still talking. She tapped on the glass knowing she'd not phone her home. She could have rung Julien but she wanted to be alone. If she'd had a bike . . . Krim had gone off on his to a rock festival, some way from Paris. He'd suggested taking her with him, she'd hesitated for a moment; Krim had said she'd be able to walk in the country, it'd be t'riff, but Sherazade let him go off by himself saying that she didn't find the country t'riff. She'd been with Meriem to holiday camps, once in Normandy then in Auvergne; they'd been bored and besides it always rained. Every time she'd stayed in a French village she didn't want to go to but where she was sent with her sister on account of another baby coming, she thought of the grandfather's village, she always asked, 'Is Algeria a long way? Is it a long way? Why don't we go there?' Her parents didn't answer. She looked for it on a tiny globe pencil-sharpener where she had a job finding Algeria and France which was half the size of a little finger nail; finally with Meriem she said, 'There it is.' She couldn't work out the distance. They looked at the globe again and thought it wasn't so very far. Sherazade knew and so did Meriem it was no good repeating that was where they wanted to go. In the bus they were car-sick and threw up several times and arrived at the holiday camp in a miserable state. They wrote letters together finding exactly the right terms for the things they disliked but they didn't send them to anyone, and no one read them but themselves.

These last few days Sherazade had been taking books by Fromentin to the shop, for when business was slack. Julien had given them to her. Sycomore Publications had recently brought out a new edition of the water-colourist's accounts of his travels and Julien had immediately bought them for Sherazade who'd never read them. She was not in the habit of going round the second-hand bookstalls, and at the flea market she never glanced at the books that the dealers threw all anyhow on to a dirty tarpaulin. *A Summer in the Sahara* and *A Year in the Sahel* had been lying around for several days in the shop and no matter how much Zouzou shook Sherazade she never stopped reading. Zouzou was intrigued and had glanced through the first book Sherazade had started on, 'the one about the Sahara' as Zouzou put it who'd looked at the title, she'd said, 'But this stuff's not a lot of laughs why d'you read it? I prefer my comics they give me more of a kick than your Sahara stories.' Zouzou read a lot of comics that her buddies lent her, *Howling Metal, Glacial Fluid, Barbarella, Charlie* . . . She said they were t'riff but France had her doubts whether Zouzou really meant it – she showed off a lot, as France pointed out when her friend opened a copy of *Humanoïds* under the nose of a customer, just to see.

'You really read them?'

'Of course, what d'you think?'

'I think you just look at the pictures.'

'Just say I'm illiterate, an ignoramus.'

'I didn't say that.'

They were on the verge of a quarrel. A customer came in. France left Zouzou to her comic book, Sherazade to Eugène Fromentin's Sahara and went to serve the young woman who was looking for some safari-style slacks, sort of leopard-skin pattern or more sort of camouflage and almond-green with spots like the paras wear but not too military with pockets and zips on the

184

thighs and ankles and well you know the sort of thing I mean. France listened patiently. She knew exactly what sort of slacks the customer meant. She'd put a pair in the window that very morning. They would be exactly right providing her size wasn't sold out, she was a comfortable 42. France looked at the customer, gave her the correct size, let her look at herself in the mirror which made you seem slightly thinner, and pat her thighs and behind to see if they fitted tightly enough without making her seem heavy ... France said nothing. The customer continued twisting and turning going from one mirror to another. France made a little sign to Zouzou and Sherazade. Finally she took the money and told Zouzou she'd have the next one.

Sherazade hadn't phoned anyone. The call box remained empty for a long time but she'd forgotten. She took the road map of Algeria out of her bag and unfolded it on the pavement in front of her. People walking near the curb, with their heads bent, stopped just in time to avoid treading on the map, and had to walk round behind the bench, as Sherazade didn't worry about leaving room for them to pass. She remembered the names she was looking for on the map and cursed because she couldn't find them.

'Can I help you, mademoiselle?'

A man had sat down next to her on the bench. She hadn't noticed him, as she leaned over the map spread out on the pavement.

'You're looking for something?'

She thought the man might be a cop. You couldn't always spot cops in plain clothes in Paris. They dressed cool – as they'd been trained to do at the Quai des Orfèvres and Sherazade was suspicious every time a man spoke to her, like this fellow. She didn't reply.

'I know this country well.'

Sherazade turned to look at the man. He smiled at her. He must have been about the same age as her father and dressed like him, not expensively but clean, neat shirt, tie, polished shoes.

'Can I have a look?'

They bent over the map together. The man showed Sherazade the place he came from and he was the one who found the grandfather's village that she'd just been looking for. He showed her where the Revolution had started. He showed her the *willayas* and talked to her about the war. He'd taken part in the start of the rebellion then he'd come to France with some others to set up networks. He'd been in the Santé Prison for several months. He said he often came back to this neighbourhood to walk round the outside of the prison, without really knowing why; he knew all the chestnut trees in the Boulevard Arago. He found himself retracing the clandestine routes that the networks had set up in Paris, and he might cover twelve to fifteen miles in this way on a Saturday or Sunday

186

afternoon without getting tired.

Sherazade listened to the man. Passers-by had trodden on the map which she'd left open in front of the bench.

Suddenly there was a sound of sirens; police cars, black marias, squads of cops on the boulevard. No demo was anticipated. Sherazade and the man were caught in a police cordon. A bank on the other side of the boulevard had just been attacked or was being attacked, no one quite knew and the cops who were checking the papers of everyone caught in this round-up set up on the spur of the moment because of the hold-up couldn't say exactly what was happening. The man took Sherazade's arm and stood with her behind the phone box.

There were shots, shouts.

The cops asked the man for his papers and he took them out of the inside pocket of his navy-blue Tergal jacket. The cop looked at them while keeping an eye on the hold-up. An ambulance arrived, the cop said, 'And the young lady?'

'She's my daughter,' replied the man.

'You can go.'

Oum Kalthoum

Julien had found out by chance where Sherazade worked. He was walking in the Halles at a time when he wasn't often there and passing the window of the dress-shop he thought he recognized Sherazade. First he saw France then Zouzou. He stopped and spotted Sherazade in one of the boutique's red and gold dresses, colours that showed up her looks to better advantage than the putty-coloured raincoat she'd brought back from the flea market and which she sometimes wore to be inconspicuous, especially when she had to travel by Metro, she explained, as she tied the neutral belt of this neutral garment which she disliked. She was wearing the red and gold Barbès scarf and while she worked kept on a walkman with red and gold headphones, the colours of the boutique. The manageress lent them to the assistants to promote them at the same time as her clothes.

The customers always asked where they could get similar ones . . . it always worked.

Julien didn't tell Sherazade he'd caught sight of her. He knew where he could see her, meet her if necessary, that was sufficient.

He was a bit late getting home after work. He wasn't thinking of Sherazade. He hadn't seen her for the last few days and she didn't ring. He knew he wouldn't hear her voice on the answerphone in the evenings when he listened to the messages. He'd worked on the scenario and the dialogue with his friend who wanted to see Sherazade and do a screen test. Julien promised every time to bring her with him next time, but his friend saw him arrive alone every time.

'Does your Sherazade really exist?'

'Yes, you've seen the photos.'

'That doesn't prove anything . . . If it's going to be like that when we start shooting . . . We can't be running after her all the time. On the whole I prefer working with professional actresses . . . they at least leave the numbers of three answering machines instead of just one so you know where to find them and you never know where this chick is.'

'That's true.'

Julien didn't switch on the light straight away. It was dark, but with the shutters open he could see well enough.

He went into the living-room to put on an opera. He hadn't been listening to music

189

recently and was missing it. A Monteverdi opera, that's what he'd listen to, lying on the single bed, before going to the Oriental concert in honour of Oum Kalthoum, which he'd have liked to take Sherazade to. He heard a sort of faint moan. He upset a full ashtray.

Sherazade was sitting in the wicker armchair with her back to the window, hugging her knees which she'd drawn up under her chin. Julien didn't switch on the light. He came over to her and knelt down near the armchair. She didn't lift her head. She didn't move, she must have been sitting like this for hours, Julien thought. Her hands were cold, slightly damp. She must have been crying.

Julien called her name softly, 'Sherazade! Sherazade!'

She didn't reply. He called her name again and stood up not knowing what to do just to make her say something, to make her move just a little, to convince himself he was doing the right thing to stay here with her. He stroked her hair, her tight soft curls. He repeated, 'Sherazade. Sherazade, talk to me.'

'No, you talk to me.'

'I can only tell you I love you, Sherazade, and that I don't want you to be unhappy, and that your coming here means a lot to me even if you don't stay, and that I only exist when I'm with you . . . and that I love you, Sherazade.'

Julien bent over Sherazade who looked at him.

So much distress . . . He had no idea why. He wouldn't ask. He lifted her up in his arms. He held her tight.

'Would you like a grapefruit with lots of sugar?'

Julien carried her to the bed, turning round like in a film, and laid her down.

'Yes, a grapefruit with lots of sugar.'

Before he went to the kitchen, he picked up his tape-recorder lying on the floor next to the armchair. He saw it had a tape in it, half recorded, but didn't think Sherazade had been using it.

'Would you like to go and hear a Tunisian singer? Zima Tounssia?'

'Whereabouts?'

'In Nogent, a concert for Oum Kalthoum.'

Sherazade leapt up.

'This evening? Can we go? You've got tickets?'

'Enrico gave me two.'

'Terrif. I'll get dressed.'

She put on a red dress that France had lent her, soft clinging silk, low cut . . . Julien came back, carrying the glass dish with the grapefruit.

'You look stunning! Lovelier than Marilyn, a thousand times lovelier. Why don't you always dress like that?'

'Wonderful! And what about the cops?'

'What about the cops?'

'Because I haven't got my forged identity card yet. I'm still waiting for it. Pierrot's buddies are

191

seeing to it. My name'll be Rosa. Rosa Mire and I'll be eighteen, I'll be of legal age you understand. I'll have been born in Paris and be studying psycho. So now you know.'

'And your nationality?'

'I'm Algerian.'

'But on your forged card, what'll you be?'

'It'll be false. I'll be French.'

She finished lacing up the open sandals with gold thongs that Zouzou had brought back from the flea market. They were too big for Zouzou. She'd tried to prove they fit her by wearing them for a whole morning in the shop . . . Sherazade had taken them. She had to give them back soon for a party. France would need them. She took off the emerald earrings and replaced them with a pair made out of tiny rare feathers that Zouzou collected. They were very fragile and Zouzou never stopped telling Sherazade to take extreme care of them.

Julien was dazzled. He repeated, 'What a beauty . . .'

'Oh, stop it . . . That's enough. Let's go!'

As they left Sherazade picked up her putty-coloured raincoat.

'Oh, no! You're not going to wear that!'

'You always forget the cops . . .'

'And you think about them all the time . . .'

'No choice.'

In the old red Volkswagen convertible, Julien said to Sherazade, 'What about going to the sea?'

'I've never seen the sea.'

'No?'

'I've seen it from the plane. My grandfather's village is a long way from the sea. In France, my parents don't travel. For the holidays I used to go to the country with my sister, we didn't see the sea.'

'We'll go now, straight away, if you like.'

'When I've got my papers, the forged ones. When my name's Rosa.'

'I prefer Sherazade.'

'I also call myself Camille. You didn't know? Depends who I'm with.'

At the concert of Oriental music, the audience went hysterical. All the Arabs from Paris and up to thirty miles around were there. Men and women with babies in their arms and youngsters grouped according to their generation and their housing estate. Youngsters were clapping and dancing in front of the podium. Girls dressed in 'Halles' fashion or rock, had taken off the scarves they wore round their necks and tied them round their behinds to do a belly dance in jeans, imitation leather miniskirts or baggy trousers. They danced like the women at an Arab celebration, in a room of the flat, among themselves apart from the men. They were dancing in public, unashamedly, knowing no one was looking at them, protected by the ring of youngsters, boys and girls, which separated them from those who might be their parents and close relatives.

They danced in twos and threes, surprised at their own daring and laughing as their shoulders, belly, buttocks quivered in the dance. Sherazade danced. Julien watched her.

Suddenly he saw Sherazade stop short, freeze, look round as if being followed. He moved over to her, wrapped her in her raincoat and led her to a spot where the light was not so bright. It had occurred to Sherazade that if all the Arabs from Paris and the surrounding suburbs were there, her parents might be present. Her mother liked Oum Kalthoum and often listened to him.

She'd have liked to catch sight of Meriem in the crowd.

She was just leaving when she heard someone call her name.

Omar

It was Omar and the gang. Sherazade told Julien to wait for her, she'd be back. She left with them. They'd turned up at the concert but got bored and were leaving again.

When she passed Julien's Volkswagen she left a note on a Metro ticket tucked under the windscreen-wiper. 'I feel better now. S.' She sat side-saddle behind Omar who wouldn't let her drive. She insisted she knew how . . . he took a look at her dress and Sherazade said, 'Oh yes, you're right . . . it's a bit tight . . . the next time you'll see.'

Omar stopped near the Gare du Nord, the gang's meeting place. He lit up a Marlboro, they all smoked American cigs that the Algerians from Algeria called *Sonaposes* – on analogy with *Sonatrac** and all the *Sociétés Nationales* which

* *Société Nationale de Transport et de Commercialisation des Hydrocarbures*, National Society for Transport and Marketing of Hydrocarbon. (Trans.)

had given rise to all the *Sonas* . . . It had become old-hat, almost common, the sign of an ex-serviceman to smoke Gauloises. No one in the gang would dare light up one in front of the others, they'd rather be seen dead than smoking cheap crummy French cigs . . . Omar said, 'I've had it up to here hanging around every week-end . . . What about a bit of fresh air . . . Should we go to Deauville, and try our luck at the Casino?'

'Where's Deauville?' Sherazade asked, pulling up the thongs of her sandals.

'It's at the seaside and there's gambling at the Casino. Shall we go? It's not far. You can win a lot of money and you'll see the sea if you've never seen it before.'

'How d'you know I've never seen it?'

'I just said so for no particular reason.'

Sherazade said she didn't want to go to the Casino or the seaside, she'd be getting a bike and would be going to Algeria.

'Really, you too?'

'What d'you mean, me too?'

'You want to go there? You know there aren't any pin-tables in the boondocks and even in the towns I don't think you find any, can you imagine!'

'I don't give a damn for pin-tables. That's not what I'm going for.'

'Why then?'

'I dunno. I just know I'm going. That's all.'

Omar said he and his mates were going down south on their bikes . . . They were going to arrange holidays on the coast. Some of them would get jobs crewing on yachts. 'The bourgeois like Arabs and gipsies . . . We'll milk them for the readies and split when they begin to smell a rat. Some of my mates've already had some fantastic summers . . . They had a ball with their birds, 'cos they told the skipper they'd have to bring their girlfriends or not come at all. The skippers thought there'd naturally be some nice little group-sex parties . . . but then . . . They locked themselves in their cabins and wouldn't come out again when they started making suggestions early in the evening. They let the old gits get on with their partner-swapping among themselves . . . Sometimes they came and knocked on the door they didn't open they said fuck off we're tired . . . I've done cruises like that right through the Mediterranean it was t'riff, Corsica, Tunisia, Greece, Turkey, Syria, Egypt . . . Wouldn't you like to come with me? You'll be far away, it'll be peaceful . . .'

'When I've got my bike . . . OK. 'Night.'

'You're not coming?'

'Not tonight. 'Bye!'

197

Ritz

Sherazade took the Metro. She didn't like travelling by Metro in the evening on account of the presence of the transport police. When she caught sight of any she'd walk fast and then break into a run to get above ground. She preferred to walk. She walked a great deal in Paris. She stopped at a call-box. She was going to phone Julien when, as often happened, someone tapped discreetly on the glass pane. It was a man in his fifties, camel-hair overcoat, signet-ring . . .

They both emerged simultaneously. He spoke to her politely. He was in Paris on business. He'd just arrived from the Middle East and he'd like to get to know some French people, Parisian women . . . He was very fond of this country, this city and it would be his pleasure to invite her to dinner wherever she'd like to go. He knew several good restaurants and if she accepted he'd spend a pleasant evening and most important

198

he'd be speaking this beautiful language . . .

Sherazade accepted the invitation.

He was very talkative. He went on and on. She wasn't bored. It was two a.m. He suggested they go to the Ritz. He had a room there he thought he could get one for her, if she liked, he could stay longer with her. Sherazade didn't feel like going back to sleep at the squat, or at Julien's. In the foyer of the hotel the businessman passed a group of women whom he greeted. He told her they were Arab princesses from the Gulf, on holiday in Paris. They said they'd been at the Kat', he'd understood it was a smart club, but he didn't know any more about it. Sherazade had heard Zouzou and France talk about Arab princesses who got their chauffeurs to drop them at the Katmandu in their Rolls, where they picked up birds and always gave them lavish presents, as well as handing out an astronomical amount of banknotes. And these bimbos developed a taste for petrodollars, if not for the Arab princesses that France said she found very ugly but France always exaggerated.

The businessman took a room for Sherazade adjoining his own. It would include breakfast. Sherazade found herself in a palatial room, as big as a drawing-room, with armchairs, couches . . . for how many people? She let the businessman accompany her to the door of her room; he kissed her hand and then suggested a little trip in a couple of days.

'If you're patient, in five days' time I'm leaving to spend a week in Florida, by the sea, or on one of the islands in the Caribbean, I don't know yet, I'll take you with me. I need a holiday, and perhaps you do too? What do you say?'

'I want to go to Algeria.'

'To Algeria? But you don't have any fun there . . . It's dreary. No one would think of spending a holiday there. You, a Parisian, you'd be bored to death in Algeria. I'll give you a few days to think it over. And then, if you need anything in the night, just tap on the interleading door to my room, on the left of your bed. The key is on your side and I think there is a little bolt, so you needn't worry . . . Goodnight, mademoiselle . . . What is your first name? You didn't tell me.'

'Camille,' said Sherazade who was sleepy.

'Goodnight, Camille. Sleep well. See you tomorrow.'

'Goodnight.'

Sherazade woke up at seven o'clock, asked for her breakfast, polished off everything edible to the last crumb and left the Ritz never to return.

She phoned Julien who was still at home. They arranged to meet at the Beaubourg library; it was Monday, the boutique was shut.

Chassériau

Julien and Sherazade had never spent the whole day together in Paris. Sherazade wanted to go to the Louvre to look at the *Women of Algiers*, always the same ones.

Julien suggested going to the Versailles Museum to look at the huge picture in the Algerian gallery, *The Capture of Abd al-Qadir's Retinue* by Horace Vernet, an artist who'd accompanied the armies of occupation in Algeria, around 1830. Julien spoke of the baroque confusion of the painting in reds and ochres, a tangle of French soldiers, camels, palanquins from which harem women had been thrown out and caught by their Negro servants, Arab warriors, spirited horses in embroidered caparisons, sheep, carpets, cattle . . . Sherazade repeated that she wanted to go to the Louvre to look at the *Women of Algiers* and the bathing women, that she'd only caught a glimpse of when they'd hurried past together to get to Delacroix without looking at anything else. The medley of plump white bodies of Ingres's *Turkish Bath* astonished her. You couldn't distinguish the ones in the background clearly when your eyes left the back and the highlighted nape of the neck of the naked woman in the centre foreground, a musician. Chassériau's *Esther at her Toilet* was not so overcrowded. On either side of the white woman with the naked torso, a serving-maid: a Moorish woman and a Negress carrying perfumes and jewels. Julien told Sherazade that Chassériau was born in the West Indies, his mother was a Creole, the daughter of settlers from Santo Domingo, now Haïti, and his father was the French consul in Porto Rico. He told her he was trying to get to see Baron Chassériau's private collection but he didn't know how to set about it. Sherazade also looked at Fromentin's Algerian landscapes and paused, before leaving, at Ingres's *Odalisque*. Like the musician in *The Turkish Bath*, she was wearing a turban whose silver and gold thread and tassels in the nape of her neck were clearly visible. Julien drew up for her an impressive but, he emphasized, incomplete list of odalisques from Delacroix to Renoir – who had painted some as a tribute to Delacroix – up to Matisse, whose paintings of odalisques from 1912 to 1929 Julien ticked off on his fingers – not counting drawings and sketches – naming them as they came into his head:

Odalisque in White Turban
Odalisque with Red Casket
Odalique in Lotus Position
Odalique with Magnolia
Odalisque with Green Foliage
Odalisque in Red Trousers (2)
Odalisque in Grey Trousers
Odalisque in Armchair

'Are they always naked women?' asked Sherazade, who heard the word *odalisque* for the first time.

'It's more that they're half-draped; apart from the one by Ingres, who only wears a turban, the ones I've been able to see are often dressed in sort of baggy trousers from just below the waist and sometimes a transparent blouse that lets you make out the breasts or else is cut low enough to reveal them. They're always reclining languidly, gazing vacantly, almost asleep . . . They suggest for Western artists the indolence, voluptuousness, the depraved allure of Oriental women. They were called *Odalisques* in nineteenth-century art, forgetting that an odalisque in the Ottoman Empire, the Turkish Empire, was simply a servant, a slave waiting on the women of the royal harem. If you like, we can go to the Museum of Modern Art and I'll show you some. But they're nearly all in private collections, like the Algerian women: Manet's Algerian woman, Corot's, Renoir's Algerian girl with the falcon, and then Matisse's Algerian woman . . . Matisse's is in the Museum of Modern Art.

In the afternoon Julien rummaged among his bookshelves to find the Orientalist albums that he hadn't touched for years and books he'd picked up on the second-hand stalls in Bordeaux, Aix-en-Provence, Paris. He read Sherazade a passage from Théophile Gautier's Algerian chronicles, taken out of his *Picturesque Journey to Algeria*, written about 1843:

'We think to have conquered Algiers and it is Algiers which has conquered us. Our women already wear scarves interwoven with gold, a medley of a thousand gaudy colours, which were used by the slaves in the harem, our young men adopt the camel-hair burnous . . . If this continues, in a very short time France will be Mohammedan and we shall see in our cities the white domes and minarets of mosques mingling with church steeples, as in Spain at the time of the Moors . . . '

'Apart from the Paris Mosque . . .' said Sherazade, 'there's one in Asnières, I know because my mother's friends go there to take offerings of bread and milk and to pray on Fridays, but are there any others?'

'France hasn't become "Mohammedan" . . . but I've heard some *pieds-noirs* say that France will soon be colonized by Arabs from North

Africa, the Mashreq* and the Gulf . . .'

'They're crazy, those *pieds-noirs* . . . and you believe them?'

'I do believe that France is becoming a multi-ethnic society . . . First with the Russians and the Poles from the East and if it continues with the dissidents in the USSR and Poland, in the other countries of Eastern Europe as well, but the exodus from there is less serious, and then from the South with the Italians, Spanish, Portuguese immigrants and again from the South with White and Black Africa, not to mention the West Indies and other islands still under French domination . . . Those of original French stock will become the new minority in a few decades,' Julien said with a laugh, 'and all because of girls like you.'

'Why me?'

'Because you are the ones who're going to have two-tone children, half-castes, cross-bred, adulterated offspring, bastards . . . hybrids . . . mongrels . . .'

'Me, children? I shan't have any.'

Sherazade was glancing at Delacroix's *Journal*. She paused at the account of his stay in Morocco and Algeria. Julien was having a bath, Sherazade came in with the book and sat on the bidet.

'Listen Julien, Delacroix's talking about what

* The eastern half of the Arab world. (Trans.)

we saw this morning. Shall I read it to you?'

'Yes, do. I've forgotten.'

'It's in 1847. I'll read the whole thing, even if it's a bore.

"31 January. Worked on *Women of Algiers*.

29 March. The next day resumed work on *Women of Algiers*, the Negress and the curtain she is lifting.

26 May. Worked with enthusiasm, although for short periods only, on *Women of Algiers*. Composed an interior in Oran with figures . . .

27 May. Enjoyed working on *Women of Algiers*: the woman in the foreground . . . "

Shall I go on?'

Julien explained that the *Women of Algiers* in the Louvre dated from 1834 and that Delacroix had taken the same subject for another smaller picture, exhibited at the 1849 Salon. It could be seen in a museum in Montpellier.

Sherazade went on:

' "5 February. Baudelaire arrived just as I was beginning again on a little figure of an Oriental woman, lying on a sofa, commissioned by Thomas in the Rue du Bac. He told me of Daumier's difficulties in finishing. Then he started talking about Proudhon whom he admires and says is the people's idol.

His views seem among the most modern

206

and completely progressive.

Continued the little figure after he left and went back to the *Women of Algiers*.

My experience with the *Women of Algiers* is that it is very satisfying and even necessary to paint on top of the varnish. Only I shall have to find a way of preventing the subsequent layers of varnish from attacking the varnish underneath, or first varnishing on top of the first outline with a permanent varnish.

Tuesday 13 March. The doctor came about five o'clock; he upset me, he talks of using small probes. I stayed by the fire.

This morning Weil took the *Odalisque* and gave me 200 F.

Thomas, *Turkish Woman* 100 F.

Lefèbvre. *Odalisque* 150 F." '

Sherazade stopped reading. She'd read the rest in the evening, in bed or at the shop. Julien told her that Delacroix had brought back from his travels in North Africa some magnificent Oriental costumes that he never liked to lend. He needed them for his pictures and sometimes wore them for fancy-dress balls.

He recalled the grotesque fancy-dress party organized and financed by a famous couturier at the Palace Hotel. His story made Sherazade laugh. The theme was *The Arabian Nights* and the guests were shown an idiotic film about an idyll worthy of *Nous deux* in the courtyards and

Moorish chambers of Moroccan palaces, with clips of the desert.

He added that at this Parisian Arabian Nights party he'd seen African princesses and Moroccan princesses, sisters of the king, two of the five officially recognized by Mohammed V, four since the accidental death of one. They were the centre of attraction and the one in the round red hat with a green feather was particularly conspicuous. The whole evening they never left their chairs nor the table on the platform reserved for VIPs. They stared at everything that moved in front of them with that royal gaze that sees no one but is there to be seen, almost like a divinity. They were accompanied by two men who talked together. They were dignified in their boredom.

Julien had been momentarily fascinated to watch a monumental woman, an extremely beautiful African princess who wore a long white gown of real ermine; the white muslin sleeves and the low-cut bodice prevented her from fainting from the heat or simply from sweating profusely. She talked on her left in an African language to a man in a dinner-jacket and on her right in French to another man, also in a dinner-jacket. Around her neck she wore a diamond necklace and Julien wondered if this woman mightn't simply be the Empress Bokassa. He never found out. Next day he'd completely forgotten these princesses of one evening.

'If you like,' said Julien, 'we can go and see Delacroix's studio it's in the Place Furstenberg in Saint-Germain.'

Sherazade began to laugh.

'Why are you laughing?'

'Because if I agreed to do what everyone's always suggesting I do . . . Anyway, with you it's not too far . . . Versailles, Saint-Germain . . . OK. Was it you who mentioned the Cotentin Peninsula to me?'

'No.'

'Then who was it?'

'How should I know? Can't you find out for yourself?'

'OK, Keep your hair on.'

Julien got up noisily, splashing Sherazade who rushed out of the bathroom with a yell. She'd switched on her walkman. Julien realized he wouldn't be able to listen to France Musique or a Verdi opera he'd just bought. He handed Sherazade a catalogue. It was of a Matisse retrospective exhibition of 1956.

'What's this?'

'Look and see. Your walkman doesn't stop you reading, I suppose.'

'No. But nobody tells me what to read.'

'OK.'

Julien took back the catalogue, sat down in the armchair and read to himself, as one studies a telephone directory or a catalogue from *La*

Redoute, Les Trois Suisses, La Camif* when you're
put out and calm your nerves by meticulously
scrutinizing a printed page, any printed matter,
concentrating on the minutest detail, careful not
to omit anything and if you do to go back over
what you missed out. So he read, while Sherazade sat at his drawing-table in the bedroom,
writing to Driss in prison, but Julien didn't
know what she was doing and he mustn't ask
her . . . He didn't like her sitting at his table
writing in her little notebooks or her private
letters while he was there. She could do that at
any other time, waiting till he'd gone . . . but no.
He got up, shut the bedroom door, sat down
again in the wicker armchair and read:

> *The Palm Leaf, Tangiers* (1912)
>   Oil on canvas. 118 × 80 cm.
>   Signed bottom right.
>   Private collection, New York.

> *Still Life with Oranges* (1912)
>   Oil on canvas. 94 × 84 cm.
>   Pablo Picasso collection.

* All mail-order catalogues. The first two for the general
public. *CAMIF – Coopérative d'Achat Mutuelle d'Instituteurs
de France*, a cooperative for the sole benefit of teachers in
government posts. (Trans.)

Moroccan Woman (1912)
    Oil on canvas. 36 × 28 cm.
    Grenoble Museum.

Moroccan Men (1916)
    Oil on canvas, 178 × 281 cm.
    Signed bottom right.
    Museum of Modern Art, New York.

The Green Gandoura (1916)
    Oil on wooden panel. 32 × 23 cm.
    Signed top left.
    Private collection, New York.

Reclining Nude with Turban (1921)
    Oil on canvas. 38 × 62 cm.
    Signed top right.
    Marcel Mabille Collection, Brussels.

The Moorish Screen (1922)
    Oil on canvas. 115 × 96 cm.
    Signed bottom right.
    The Philadelphia Museum of Art.

Odalisque with Magnolia (1924)
    Oil on canvas. 65 × 81 cm.
    Signed bottom right.
    Mr and Mrs Leigh B. Block Collection, Chicago.

Odalisque with Red Casket (1927)
  Oil on canvas. 51 × 65 cm.
  Signed and dated bottom left.
  Private collection.

The Negress (1952–53)
  Gouache pasted on canvas. 450 × 625 cm.
  No date or signature.
  Private collection.

Matisse had made several visits to Morocco from 1911 onwards.

Auteuil

Before it got dark, Julien and Sherazade had gone round to the Auteuil Gardens which Sherazade had no idea existed, and which Julien had got to know recently thanks to a botanist friend who worked at the Museum of Natural History. So he'd learnt that they taught horticulture there, training the best gardeners in Paris. The gardens were frequently deserted; Parisians preferred the dusty woods where their dogs could have a run while their owners could keep in trim as well. You were allowed into the exotic conservatories, which was not possible in the Botanical Gardens, but they were hot and humid and you couldn't sit for long on the green-painted iron seats.

Sherazade in jeans, with her Adidas and leather blouson, didn't immediately suggest odalisques or Algerian women . . . Sherazade wasn't thinking about them. She saw Julien smile as he

213

looked at her, but didn't wonder why. When he smiled like that she knew he was happy.

'What about taking some shots for the film here, in one of the conservatories?'

'No way!'

'Why? It's beautiful.'

'It's so beautiful that you see it all the time in fashion adverts, boutiques or commercials for Club Méditerrannée and that sort of thing . . . local colour. So no way.'

'You're right. I hadn't thought about that.'

'You're always a hundred years behind the times with what you think, that's for sure.'

'Charming as usual . . . We won't come here any more or rather I won't come to Auteuil to the gardens again with you.'

'If it's for the film, you can come without me.'

Meriem

It was Thursday, dressmaking day. Sherazade's mother, who did sewing at home, had decreed, for her friends and all the women of the family known as cousins, a convenient word which covered every degree of relationship, that Thursday would be Dressmakers' Day. They all did a little sewing and on that day the flat became a workshop. Each woman arrived with her light equipment and her dress lengths; some of them had up to ten dresses on the go at once; they settled down and chatted, they cut out, adjusted, assembled, tried on, and the whole business without a pattern, without a magazine, just using their eyes. Sherazade and Meriem were allowed among the women on those afternoons, as their mother thought they would learn by watching and listening.

The Thursday dresses were always for special occasions. They would be made in preparation for a wedding, a circumcision, the Feast of Eïd. It wasn't done to wear the same dress twice when you often met the same women, and then at these festivities you had to change several times a day. You arrived with a suitcase or a big bag in which the dresses were carefully folded. They could be shown off. Whatever were the latest materials to reach the Arab traders in Barbès or Montmartre became the fashion. The following week all the women wore the same material but the style varied according to the dressmaker. They were always lovely light materials with a sheen, in golds or silvers and with floral motifs printed on a background the colour of a pansy or a rose. The style was simple, nearly always gathered in at the waist with elastic and the dress would have full sleeves and ankle-length skirt. The bodice, whether high or low-necked, would be embroidered with beads, sequins and intricate insertions forming arabesques. When the women purchased the material, they would buy at the same time several belts and the scarf or shawl to go with it. Much care was also lavished on sequinned waistcoats to be worn for special occasions. On these Thursdays, they sewed in Arabic for an Arab fashion using Arab materials that were only worn by immigrant women from the Maghreb. Over the years, Sherazade and Meriem, who always managed to salvage scraps of the finest and most iridescent materials, had heard repeated hundred of times,

216

on Thursdays then on feast days, the names of the materials which were scattered around the flat, until the moment when the husband came home; then everything vanished, with a speed which always astonished the two sisters, and the place was as tidy as if no one had been there all day. The women had worked, sewed, chatted, laughed, drunk the tea prepared by Meriem and Sherazade, mint tea. *Sateen crêpe, muslin, bouclé, Champs-Elysée, Chadli* material ... Sherazade and Meriem knew exactly what each of these names suggested, the colours, the motifs, the ease in handling or the degree of transparency and even the style of the dress. For example, *Chadli** material had been all the vogue at one time; supple and light, the material fell easily into great long petals each of which could form one panel of a skirt. They were familiar with the jewels worn on special occasions and knew that every woman, just like their mother who wore nearly all of them to show them off, would be carrying with her two to three million old francs' worth of gold jewellery.

They looked forward excitedly to the luxury of those red-letter days when the women's songs and dances, and cries as well, allowed them to forget the dreary neutral grey of the other days,

* Just as 'Champs-Elysée' suggests the wealth and the smart shops of Paris, so 'Chadli' – the name of the President of the Algerian Republic – suggests something costly and superior, fit for a President's family. (Trans.)

217

when they dressed Western fashion in a country where it nearly always rains.

On Thursdays, in the women's apartments, preparations were made for the profusion of colours, the resplendence of Arab festivities.

On the Thursday when Meriem's mother had decided to make her an Arab dress in apple-green muslin for the wedding of a first cousin, her friends came to sew also for their daughters of marriageable age. The mothers worked faster and better than the daughters who preferred to read photo-romances which Meriem's mother found after the sewing afternoons and threw away immediately before one of her girls made off with them, which was known to occur. They had nothing else to read at home except the newspaper which their father brought back from work, usually *France-Soir*.

Meriem's mother was telling a story when her daughter beckoned to her from the door. The mother indicated that this wasn't the moment to interrupt her for nothing and went on with the story and the dressmaking. She was oversewing the apple-green muslin that Meriem had climbed on the table to try on for the hem. A very skilled embroiderer, that all the mothers vied with each other to get for their daughters' trousseaux, was going to embroider the slightly *décolleté* bodice: green beads would form a sort of frieze like bunches of bottle-green grapes. She would use the same beads on the sash and around the edge of the head-scarf, also green, paler than the green of the dress but the same shade. Green, the women said among themselves, was the colour of Algeria.

Meriem insisted. The other women mustn't see her. The mother decided to join her daughter in the kitchen; she said she was going to make fresh coffee, so as not to arouse suspicions. Meriem showed her mother the special envelope that didn't seem just to contain a letter. Several perhaps? The mother took out the cassette, turned it over without quite understanding. She was used to the cassettes of Arab songs that her sons often gave her, but this one intrigued her. She looked at Meriem.

'Sherazade sent it . . .'

The mother understood, put her arms round the daughter she hadn't lost and hugged her tightly as if she was hugging two at once, as she often used to do when they were small: they were the same size although Meriem was the older of the two girls. The mother hid the cassette in the pocket of her skirt, under the dress with the tiny floral pattern, and made fresh coffee for her friends. She knew they wouldn't leave before the usual time.

'Patience,' she said to Meriem who would have liked to chase her mother's friends away immediately.

But after the friends, there would be the father, the brothers, the little sisters, when would the two of them be able to listen to the cassette, hear Sherazade, if it was her speaking? There was no name on the cassette, but it had been sent to Anna-Maria, as arranged.

Towards evening, when the little ones had been bathed and put to bed, and the sons and the father were in front of the telly, Meriem called her mother into the bathroom for a henna. No one would disturb them. The mother took the little tape-recorder, fingered the cassette in her pocket and they shut themselves in for Meriem's henna.

It was Sherazade's voice.

The mother stopped, a lock of hair in her left hand, the right one full of henna.

Sherazade was talking. To her mother. To Meriem.

The mother resumed her dyeing with her accustomed skill and wept as she listened to her daughter. The tears fell on to Meriem's hair and the henna flakes. Meriem did not weep. She said to her mother, 'Cry, Imma, cry if you want to.'

Sherazade didn't say where she was or what she was doing. She talked like one writes a letter. Neither time or place mattered. She could have been talking the previous evening, or three months before, you couldn't tell.

Sherazade's voice was calm, almost affectionate. She spoke about her father, her brothers, her little sisters, to her mother and sister who listened to her voice.

When the henna was finished, Sherazade was sending kisses to them all. The mother said, 'My daughter is alive . . .'

And she gave thanks to Allah.

Châtelet

Sherazade went out to post her letter to Driss but didn't come back that evening or all that night. Julien found a note like she often left, as she never phoned except to say I'm coming and then not very often ... On a scrap torn off an envelope that Julien didn't discover till next morning, she'd written, 'I'm not an odalisque.' Most times she didn't sign. Shit, thought Julien and went to his computor. Fortunately the programme was complicated. He wouldn't think about Sherazade. He thought about her all day and waited for her till evening.

Sherazade took the Metro, without being sure where she was going. Every time she saw graffiti in Arabic script on a poster, she took out a Chinese notebook kept for the purpose, and carefully jotted down the words, the expressions she wasn't quite sure of, checked, after copying them, that she hadn't made a mistake, forgotten a sign or a curlicue. She noted which station, whether the advertisement was for a commercial product or a film, how far along the platform. She noticed more and more graffiti in Arabic script now she wanted to take them all down . . . Once she was carefully copying several lines in Arabic and when she got to the last one she saw written in roman capitals underneath the Arabic inscription – slogan? poem? song? insults? – UNKNOWN LANGUAGE . . . She couldn't understand these inscriptions until Julien managed to read and translate what she'd copied. In general, it was a question of political slogans against autocratic regimes in one or other of the Arab countries, slogans for the freeing of political prisoners arbitrarily detained, slogans for the defence of Human Rights everywhere in the world, for the Palestinians against the Israeli occupation . . .

She'd got out at Châtelet station and before leaving she'd once again taken down some Arabic wording. She was closing her notebook when she heard shouts at the other end of the platform. A woman was screaming, 'Stop them! stop them!' Sherazade saw a crowd gather and was jostled by a squad of uniformed cops who arrived at the double. She immediately followed them, forgetting her usual caution; she was putting herself at risk. She got close to the group but couldn't see what was going on. From the comments she overheard, she realized two pick-pockets had been caught red-handed by a small party of plain-clothes inspectors who'd been following them for several hours, from station to station . . . The inspectors had brought it off, if there were a few more like them, as keen and energetic, the Metro would be a safer place and you wouldn't be mugged by these hooligans who came in now direct from the suburbs on the RER and spent all day in the Metro corridors in central Paris, on the lookout for easy prey, women, old men, scared youngsters yes there were still some well brought-up children among this generation . . . And then if you kept them in prison longer but they were let out immediately, they weren't even recorded and when they did go to prison, they always got out quicker and quicker what's more soon the prisons'd be putting out red carpets to welcome them what with these reforms the new minister was preparing, the one who'd done away with capital punishment . . . Of course you wouldn't have insisted on the guillotine for them these young pickpockets like you wouldn't go as far as that but what you ought to do they ought to be sent back where they came from let them try that in their own country, they'd have their hands and ears cut off and maybe hanged in public, they'd see whether in France . . . Sherazade tried to make her way through these opinions of the French Metro users, and get closer. Why was she trying to see them? If the cops checked all the young-sters standing around she'd got her residence permit but what if the police had her descrip-tion? She didn't think they would have. By what she'd managed to hear, the two lads were young immigrants. She thought, without putting her suspicions into words, that possibly Krim or Basile . . . They were the ones she was thinking of. She had to know for sure. The uniformed cops surrounded the inspectors who were put-ting the cuffs on the two lads. They were going up the escalator when Sherazade shouted, with-out thinking, 'Omar! Omar!'

Omar turned round, recognized Sherazade and, lifting his hands held in the cuffs, shouted, 'We'll meet over there!'

Omar was with one of his mates she'd already seen in the gang. He was a half-caste and like Basile wanted to go to Africa, to Senegal. His father was French, his mother Senegalese. Brought up in France in his father's family, he hadn't seen his mother for a long time. But he wasn't stealing to pay for his trip, he'd already got his ticket, he'd told her the last time they'd met. He'd even showed it to his pals.

Omar and Martial had disappeared at the top of the escalator with the escort. A journalist who was accompanying the inspectors had taken a number of pictures of the lads.

Sherazade just missed an identity check.

She went up to the Halles Forum, with the crush on the escalators. She wanted to warn Zouzou and France who knew Omar and Martial well, but instead of leaving the Metro, she found herself on level four which led to the RER platforms for the suburban lines. She'd been following an Algerian family from the escalators on to the platforms, waiting for the train that the father, mother carrying a baby, and the five little girls had got into to leave.

Sherazade had caught sight of a man in the distance, in his fifties, wearing a beige raincoat and black patent shoes, who was carefully carrying a big box of cakes, it must have held a dozen. He was holding the hand of a little girl of about two and a half whose other hand was held by her three- or four-year-old sister. The two older sisters walked behind the father, nine-year-old twins who chattered away without paying any attention to their sister who was waiting rather anxiously for the mother . . . The mother was a young woman in her thirties in a green pleated skirt and long acrylic jacket; she had a heavy baby asleep in her arms. She walked slowly and the father frequently turned round especially when they got to the escalators on to which the whole family had to be dragged all together, some of them laughing, some apprehensive. Sherazade was watching the box of cakes that she kept thinking was going to upset when the father picked up the smallest little girl to jump off at the end of the escalator.

On the platform the mother checked to see that the twins had still got hold of the big Tati bag that they were almost dragging and which pulled them down on one side. Sherazade was quite close to the family and watched and listened. None of them paid any attention to her. They were completely engrossed in the long journey by Metro.

In the rush for the train, one of the little girls who'd let go of her sister's hand, was nearly left behind on the platform. The passengers were pushing and shoving. Sherazade just had time to pick up the child and put her down next to her mother on the step of the train. The young woman looked at Sherazade and smiled at her through the glass pane of the door as it slammed. She had blue tattoos between her eyes.

Esther

Sherazade walked along the Rue du Faubourg-Saint-Denis to visit France and Zouzou. In the window of a fashion boutique called NOW she saw a little notice; she stopped to read it:

Situation Vacant
Dress-designer and Pattern-cutter
'Young styles'
Able to assemble patterns

She nearly went in to ask for information but thought better of it. She'd ask Zouzou first what training a dress-designer and pattern-cutter needed. At the main entrance it occurred to her that her friends might have gone out, they rarely spent the evening at home.

She rang. A tall black girl with a frizzy Afro opened the door. She heard Zouzou shout, 'Who is it?'

'It's me, Sherazade.'

'Oh! Hi! D'you know Esther?'

Her name was Esther, she was African, a journalist in exile in Paris.

'Prohibited from entering her own country,' France explained for the benefit of Zouzou who hadn't the slightest interest in politics. Esther was thirty and worked at Radio France International. With some other women, she was responsible for an Afro-Caribbean magazine. She'd met France at an African evening and they'd seen each other again at meetings for the Franz Fanon Memorial.

'Come and look, Sherazade! This is teriff.'

Zouzou was surrounded by her new salvage-acquisitions and was trying things on in front of the mirror propped against the wall. Everything was jumbled together: pink and green plastic mini-skirts, some straight some flounced, flat sequined dance-shoes, Levi 501s, blouses with frilly collars – what d'you call them, pirate or corsair-style? – spray-cans of coloured lacquer – you could turn your hair green, orange, blue, silver, gold, Zouzou was giving herself a gold slightly frizzed hair-do, explaining it would wash out first time – American butterfly specs, a fluorescent green heart, a transparent suitcase, a pink and green fluorescent purse, fluorescent earrings that Zouzou had been wearing all day of so vivid a pink they made France scream, Eskimo key-rings, boxing gloves . . .

229

'Your place is a real shop,' Sherazade said, trying on a threadbare machine-made leather jacket that had been given to one of Zouzou's buddies but after a week he'd decided it was really too shabby, grotty. He preferred a biking jacket in padded leather with over-stitching that Sherazade already envied without ever having seen it.

Esther and France glanced from time to time at Zouzou who was dressing up to the appropriate music; hard rock, Police, Telephone, Blondie, Higelin, Lavilliers, Bashung, Chagrin d'amour . . . They were talking about political groups that Zouzou didn't know and didn't want to know. Zouzou was saying, 'When I hear "Third World", "Undeveloped, Under-development" . . . I reach for my revolver . . .'

France and Zouzou often argued because France accused Zouzou of being permanently corrupted by *Babylon* and she wouldn't be surprised to find her a hostess in a bar, then ending up as a call-girl and . . . Zouzou would cut her short, shrieking, 'I can have a ball if I like and live my own life and be super-cool without crying all the time over the immigrants, the Third World and all that . . . Anyway politics isn't going to feed me.'

France said it didn't matter if she didn't understand it wouldn't stop her being happy. She wasn't the only one who didn't understand there were some people in the world who cared passionately about justice and liberty and that was what made them tick and she wasn't the only one to always be running such people down . . . Zouzou interrupted her diatribe. 'But I'm free, I am, and I don't ask anybody for anything, nobody helps me, I've fought for what I've got, what d'you think . . .'

'And the others?'

'They can do like me and anyway stop bugging me you always have to spoil everything with your preaching about militating when you don't even militate yourself and you get worked up about nothing and after all you don't turn up your nose at all the parties and idiotic pals . . .'

Zouzou, in a fury, started stamping on all the things she'd spread out in front of the mirror, still in her winkle-pickers that she'd just laced up over pink tights of a lighter shade than the flounced mini-skirt that she'd put on a short time ago with a green sequinned blouse, as bright as her fluorescent earrings. France let her carry on. Esther and Sherazade watched her, wondering if she was going to spare the records.

Esther suggested she take them all to see her magazine. Zouzou, always ready for an excuse to change her outfit, agreed enthusiastically. It was near the Bastille.

In a café where they stopped after the magazine, Sherazade told them about Omar and Martial getting arrested at Châtelet station.

231

Zina

Esther had put Sherazade up for the night. She lived alone in a large one-room flat where working meetings were often held for the magazine. She didn't ask Sherazade any questions but talked about herself late into the night.

As she left, Sherazade told Esther she'd come and see her again.

'Are you interested in the magazine?'

'I write poems.'

'Will you send me some?'

'If you like.'

Sherazade was late. Dropping in at the library in the morning, she'd caught sight of Julien sitting in his usual place. She tiptoed in and threw her arms round his neck. He jumped. She kissed him behind his ear and said hello. He told her he had to meet his film-director friend about seven o'clock. She could come on later if she liked. He gave her the address.

Sherazade hurriedly rummaged in her pockets for the name of the street and the number. She put her walkman on again.

When she arrived they were going over the dialogue of the script. Sherazade had had her hair cut at Rocky's where Zouzou had a pal who'd got the boss to make reductions for her friends and Sherazade had taken advantage of this. Her emerald earrings showed up better; you also noticed her ears now; they were small with nice curled little rims. She was wearing the 501s that Zouzou had lent her – they were supposed to be worn short but they were really too short for Sherazade – over her red sequinned stockings and the sequinned waistcoat that was concealed by the threadbare leather jacket. She'd found an embroidered muslin blouse at Josselyne's in the flea market – just the right size – that suited her perfectly.

'That's her! That's Zina!' exclaimed Julien's friend as soon as he saw her. 'I've been on the look-out for ages, ever since the first film I've had the idea of a girl like this. You're brilliant Julien. A scenario and the heroine at the same time ... I've seen lots of girls ... It didn't necessarily have to be someone pretty, especially not a cover-girl ... but all the ones who turned up thought they were obliged to look like fashion models or girls in commercials or film stars. Eventually they all became trivial, insipid, boring and there I was thinking every time I was going to find the one who got away from all the stereotypes, rather like the actress in my first film. Finally, as none of them fitted my idea of my heroine, I thought – the first one with green eyes, but really green, not grey-green or blue-green . . . it was ridiculous as girls with green eyes really do exist and I wasn't necessarily going to get exactly what I wanted. Not a single one turned up. I gave it up. I decided I'd leave it to chance. I didn't look for anyone for weeks. I did look at girls in the street, in cafés, you never know, but it was no use. And then Julien showed me some photos. I don't trust photos, unless I've taken them myself. It seemed about right but I needed to see for myself and there you are, I can see with my own eyes, Sherazade in person . . . Zina. You are Sherazade?' he asked.

'Yes.'

'And you'd like to be in films?'

'Dunno.'

'Does the girl in Julien's script appeal to you?'

'Very much.'

As Sherazade had never done a voice test, nor had an audition as actors normally do for the stage, Julien's friend tried working with the two of them straight away. They chose a scene in which the heroine had a long speech and another in which the dialogue between the girl and her bloke was difficult to say.

'I've hit on a title!'

'What?'

'We'll call it, *The Suburbs are Fine.*'

'What?' exclaimed Sherazade. 'That's incredible. That's the name of Pierrot's newspaper.'

'Who's this Pierrot?'

'A buddy who wants to bring out a newspaper or a radio station I'm not sure which and the name is *The Suburbs are Fine.*'

'This paper doesn't exist ... nor the radio station ...'

'Nor does your film ...'

'But I'm going to register the title and the scenario. I don't fancy anyone pinching it off me.'

Julien's friend had fitted out a room which impressed Sherazade. The equipment was even more up-to-date than that of her squat-mates – and that's saying something as they'd assembled in their sound-proof room the most sophisticated stuff they could find and they knew a thing or two about it ... She'd tell them what she'd seen here, she thought, without giving them the address, not really believing they'd do a break-in, not at one of her friend's – no not really ...

They spent several hours shut up in this room,

235

as artificial and bleak as a recording studio. Julien's friend was persistent, everything had to be just right, he would wear everyone out, but if they continued, by morning he'd be quite certain. He felt reassured before morning. After five hours Julien's friend told Sherazade she'd be a gang leader, rebel, poet, unruly, adept with a knife, expert at karate (like his first prostitute heroine), fearless, a fugitive from ZUPs, hanging around housing estates, basements, underground carparks, wandering the streets, as illusive and frightening as a war-leader . . . His list was endless; he was excited at having the voice, the face, the body, the girl he was looking for, this *Zina* – the name meant pretty in Arabic – who'd existed so strongly for him every since he'd read Julien's script. He'd heard of delinquent girls, gang leaders in the inner city and the outskirts of Paris, girls who were unhappy and ruthlessly made other boys and girls – as much victims as themselves – pay for everything they'd had to put up with since childhood, and it was a perpetual dog's life for everyone, that lasted until the gang dispersed or ended up in prison, or drug addiction centres, the hospital or the cemetery. They were aware of this but it didn't matter, they were terrifying as a gang and they terrified each other also, it was a game to them, it was their life.

Julien's friend had recorded Sherazade–Zina on video. Sherazade could see and hear herself for the first time on a screen. It was curious, as if it didn't concern her. The girl she was seeing wasn't her. This person interested her, but remotely. Julien's friend made some comments, so did Julien. Sherazade said nothing.

'What do you think of it?'

'Nothing.'

'I think it's fantastic . . . You really are Zina.'

Sherazade said nothing.

'I don't really know.'

'You are Zina, really, if I say so.'

'OK. I'm hungry.'

'Let's eat.'

Julien and his friend made a salad and grilled a steak. Sherazade was drinking a Coca-Cola, sitting in a huge leather armchair, an old study chair retrieved from the family property. Just as Julien arrived with the salad, she caught sight of a book on the round slatted table made of chestnut wood, she hadn't noticed till then . . . There was a picture of an Arab or Berber woman. It was called *Algerian Women 1960*. She glanced through it. Faces of women not wearing veils in front of a camera held by a French soldier, taking pictures for the census of several villages in the interior . . . these faces displayed the severity and violence of people who submit to arbitrary treatment, knowing they will find the inner strength to resist. These Algerian women all

237

faced the lens as if they were facing a machine-gun shooting them, with the same intense, savage stare, a fierceness that the picture could only file for posterity without ever mastering or dominating. These women all spoke the same language, her mother's language.

Sherazade turned the pages of the collection of photographs and in spite of herself the tears streamed down her face.

Julien's friend brought in the piping-hot steak, grilled with herbs, done to a turn, with a knob of butter. He nearly dropped the wooden tray in front of Sherazade who was weeping like one who has taken leave of her senses – softly, silently, ceaselessly. He glanced at Julien on the other side of the armchair. Julien hadn't noticed Sherazade he was waiting to eat, he was hungry.

They all sat down at their places, in front of their plates and glasses. Julien's friend cut the meat into three equal portions. Julien served the salad. They drank a Beaujolais in silence.

Sherazade said she wasn't hungry. She got up, took her jacket and left.

'So, what about Zina?' said Julien's friend.

Yasmine

At the squat Sherazade found her room occupied. Two boys from Lyons, who were on the run, had heard of the place through the bush telegraph and as the room was empty, even if Sherazade slept there some evenings, they'd made themselves at home and refused to move. Pierrot had warned them Sherazade wasn't dead, hadn't run away or gone off on her travels; they'd wait till she turned up to move into another room which might be free then. Sherazade went into the room to pick up the things she wanted to take with her. The double bed was unmade, not the single one. Sherazade wasn't any more curious about the way they lived than any of the others who hadn't looked in to see if they were sleeping in the same bed, it didn't matter a damn to any of them except the two of them, as just when Vero came with her belongings into the room they'd settled in, as there wasn't anothed bed or mattress free in the squat and she'd just quarrelled with Rachid and decided to split with him as he wouldn't even cut a little bit off his mohican or wear any other shoes than those stupid old clodhoppers that he did everything except sleep in, the Mexican boots which were completely down-at-heel and looked like leaky boats, so when Vero turned up at the door, with her arms loaded, saying there was a bed free for her and she wouldn't bother them they refused categorically to share the room with Vero even temporarily. François said he and Selim each slept in one of the beds and there was no question of changing. Vero dumped her things on the single bed and declared, without more ado, that they didn't have to play silly buggers with her, everybody knew the single bed wasn't occupied and if they both wanted to sleep or do anything else in the big one it was their own business, but for a bed to stay empty while she, Vero, had nowhere to sleep was a scandal. A veritable council meeting had to be called to resolve the question of the single bed; Pierrot knew Vero wouldn't have hesitated to fight with François or Selim if the argument had continued. It was decided that the single bed should be moved into the big communal room where Vero would be allowed to sleep when she wanted to. Rachid wasn't there the day these moves were decided on. For the moment he was alone in one room and in a double bed. He hoped it would last and even that Vero would take herself off somewhere else. She was always reproaching him, making remarks and chasing him round all evening with a pair of hair-dresser's scissors in her hand, bugging him about his mohican hair-do which was drooping over his eyes. And if he wanted to keep his mohican he was free to do so, OK? He wasn't going to let her lay down the law to him. He'd told her he wasn't going to spend his holidays with her mother in the South, no way now, she could tell her mother, he'd made up his mind and that was that. Every time Rachid mentioned these holidays which he'd screwed up, Vero did her nut and he left the others to deal with her. He'd got to beat it, he'd got to see someone urgently about a training course, he wasn't going to miss it for this shag.

Sherazade asked Pierrot to rescue her red bed-spread, she was attached to it and would need it.

Driss hadn't been discharged from prison yet and Eddy had written from Tunisia, saying he'd finally found Djamila, not in Setif where her father lived, but in the south in Ghardaïa, in a luxury hotel. He hadn't asked what she was doing there; nor who she'd come with to the Oasis Hotel . . .

He'd more or less kidnapped her.

241

Djamila hadn't really made any difficulties and so was living with Eddy in Tunisia in a little square house with a terrace all overgrown with purple and pink bougainvillaeas, overlooking the sea. In Setif, Djamila had seen her father who'd made her welcome where he lived with his new wife, but after a week Djamila had realized she couldn't stay any longer. She sent her mother a card from Setif, giving no news, simply saying she was all right. From Tunisia she wrote to her father saying she'd been pleased to see him again and perhaps she'd stay in Tunisia, that's what she'd decided with Eddy. They'd stay a year or two, Djamila would go to university and he'd make out with his music, in the summer the clubs needed musicians. Eddy told Pierrot and Basile that the house with the bougainvillaeas, which was isolated and hidden away, would make an ideal safe house for them. They just had to let him know. Sherazade could come too. Pierrot let Sherazade read the letter and she made a mental note of the address in Tunisia, forgetting that she didn't know Eddy's surname. She looked at the envelope and saw Pierrot's full name for the first time, it was Pierrot Kovalsky, like many Poles from the North of France. She'd never said what her name was either and nobody had asked her.

Sherazade heard that Pierrot and Basile were preparing a job.

'We're not going on a spree, it's political,'

Pierrot emphasized without giving any details of what it was all about . . . 'You'll see, it'll make the headlines and the lads won't stagnate in prison here or anywhere else 'cos we're not going to confine ourselves to France . . .'

'And Krim?'

'Krim's busy with his own affairs, don't worry about him, Krim won't end up in Fleury, believe me. He's hand in glove with some Japanese businessmen, you can guess what about. He's suggested some designs, he's been invited to Japan, so you can imagine, there's no holding him. "You fellers, I'm leaving you to your hand-to-mouth existence, I'm clearing off, a long way off; I've been invited to Japan, bike manufacturers who believe in what I'm doing . . . I'll come back at the head of an empire . . . you'll see . . ." He's gone. He's sent us postcards from over there. It's not phony. When Driss gets out he won't find anyone at the squat except newcomers, I don't know who, it changes all the time now. Will you write to him?'

'Yes, I'll write. But when are you leaving?'

Pierrot explained to Sherazade that he wanted to go back up north to see his family and friends before leaving in ten days or so. He told her about Yasmine.

'I want to see Yasmine again.'

'Yasmine? Do I know her?'

'No. She stayed back there. She never wanted to come to Paris.'

Pierrot showed her a Polaroid photo of Yasmine, a Moroccan born in a village near Bruay-en-Artois, to a miner's family. The father had lived there for a long time. Pierrot had got to know her through her brother Mohammed, who everyone called Momo. If you didn't see him you might think his name was Maurice. They'd known each other since primary school and had become friends at high school. Pierrot never used to go to Momo's house, but Momo spent his afternoons at Pierrot's pottering about and listening to records that he didn't have at home. Pierrot lent him books for his sister Yasmine he'd seen for the first time at the municipal library. He'd taken a fancy to her. She was a plump good-natured girl, often full of fun, and Pierrot who up till then had preferred to be in the woods, on the sportsfield or at political meetings became a regular reader at the library, where he didn't read because he chatted all the time to Yasmine. He didn't see her anywhere else. Like the Moroccan girls of her age, she didn't go out – no cinema or swimming-bath or cafés. Once, with Momo as chaperon, she'd spent a couple of hours at Pierrot's; the three of them had listened to music and chatted in his room. Pierrot's mother had brought them tea and slices of fruit-cake but didn't stay with them. When Pierrot left Bruay, they'd written to each other then suddenly Pierrot didn't hear from Yasmine any more, in spite of the letters he wrote her nearly every day. Yet she'd told him she loved him, just once, in a letter she'd given him at the library before he left for Paris.

Momo had let him know, after several months' silence, that Yasmine had been married off. He'd never seen her again, but as he was going to leave Paris, he wanted to try to speak to her. He knew she'd not left the North. Momo had made it clear she was not shut up. Perhaps she still went to the library?

Pierrot asked Sherazade if she still wanted to go to Algeria. He was leaving by car for Orleans, he could give her a lift if she was going in that direction. Sherazade asked him to phone her the day before he left, she'd have made up her mind in a few days. She left Julien's phone number, without giving his name or address.

She was leaving. Pierrot put into her right hand a tiny packet wrapped in red tissue paper. He was in a hurry. Basile was waiting for him in a bistro for a meeting.

At some red lights, Sherazade undid the tissue paper. She found earrings formed from three little rings, two in gold, one in platinum.

245

Verdi

A few days after he'd left for the North Pierrot phoned Sherazade. Julien took the message for her. Pierrot hadn't give his name. Julien handed the paper to Sherazade without any comment. Pierrot had said, 'I'll ring again at midday on Thursday.'

Julien told her, 'Thursday I'm not here . . . You'll have the place to yourself.'

Sherazade pulled a face at him, folded the message and put it in the back pocket of her jeans.

Julien worked all afternoon, shut up in his bedroom. Sherazade was listening to Verdi. She was beginning to like opera, the women's voices excited her; she told herself she'd take singing lessons as Pierrot had suggested; she'd be able

246

to sing like certain Black Americans, not only rock and all that, but opera as well. She'd enroll next month, if she didn't leave. She must hurry up if she wanted to sing properly she was already seventeen, she ought to have begun much earlier. But in the suburbs where they lived the choral societies were all Catholic and her mother wouldn't hear of it; on the other hand, she and Meriem had been accepted for the municipal folk group where they'd chosen the Alsacian and Nice groups because of the costumes. Their mother had kept the costumes and they'd often worn them to dance in at the end-of-the-year parties.

Julien had dozens of albums of operas. He knew them all and Sherazade often heard him singing in the bath. He also had records of contemporary music: experimental, sophisticated, electronic music, created by researchers at the IRCAM* who Julien sometimes worked with out of curiosity; he listened to this music with a concentration that Sherazade thought ridiculous . . . Julien flew into a rage and told her to go and listen to her crap in the underground carparks in Crimée, urban rock which was more her style, in a Tower of Babel, concrete wired for sound by dago musicians.

'I want to sing, that's what I want, to sing

* *Institut de Recherche et de Coordination Acoustique-Musique*, Institute for Research and Coordination of Acoustic Music. (Trans.)

opera and all that . . .,' said Sherazade.

'You really want to?' said Julien who'd calmed down.

'Yes.'

'And what about the film? What about Zina?'

'I can do that as well.'

Sherazade listened to Verdi to the end. Julien was still working. It must be three or four o'clock in the afternoon. She'd got time . . . She'd taken a day off from work with a sore throat. But it wasn't serious.

Sherazade took her putty-coloured mac and went out.

Sherazade

Sherazade rang Julien from a call-box in Beaubourg. She'd decided she'd wait for Pierrot at the squat, so she could leave immediately. She'd go and fetch her things from Julien's when he wasn't there, she knew more or less, she'd see.

'Hello! Julien! It's Sherazade. I'm off . . .'

'What?'

'I'm off. You heard me. I'm leaving . . .'

'Who with?'

'With Pierrot, if that's what interests you.'

'But who is this Pierrot?'

'I've already told you. A buddy. He's got a car, he's going in the Orleans direction, he's giving me a lift.'

'But you, where are you going?'

'I don't know . . . I'm going to Algeria.'

'To Algeria? Why didn't you tell me? We could've gone together. I'd really like to go there

249

with you. You know that, I told you once, and you know I was born in Nedroma, besides . . .'

'Besides what?'

'Besides, besides . . . nothing. Anyway, you're kidding. If you like we can leave straight away. I'll drop everything, I'll leave with you. We'll go to Orly and go by plane. Will you? Sherazade . . .'

'I want to go to Algeria alone, ALONE, you understand.'

'But this bloke, Pierrot that you're going with?'

'I've told you; I dunno where he's going; I'm going with him as far as Orleans, that's all. Afterwards I'll see.'

'You can go there alone and I'll join you there. That's possible, isn't it?'

'No.'

'When are you leaving?'

'Tomorrow.'

'Shall I see you this evening?'

'Dunno.'

That night Sherazade slept with Julien. But Julien was unhappy. He woke her several times to look at her. As they made love, Sherazade had said she loved him, and he didn't believe her.

Sherazade was the first up.

She looked at Julien as he slept. She'd told him she loved him, just once, and he hadn't believed her. She knelt down near the bed and kissed him on the corner of his eye where it's soft just before

250

the beard begins, and stroked his shoulder, he always slept naked. Julien sighed with satisfaction, without waking.

Sherazade went down to have a coffee.

Julien had an appointment at nine o'clock. Sherazade kept an eye on the clock in the café. At nine fifteen she went back up to get her things. Julien had left.

In the big bag she put:

Her red panties nicked from the Monoprix stores.

No bra she has small round breasts.

White T-shirts, short ones for daytime, long ones for night.

A blue and white Norwegian pullover that Julien often lent her.

A pair of jeans, Levis.

Two pairs of socks, white bouclé cotton.

A red towel belonging to Julien, who's got plenty more.

Paper handkerchiefs good quality.

The white burnous taken from her mother's cupboard.

In a little white leather case belonging to Julien, that she finds convenient for toilet things, she put:

·*A tube of toothpaste*, Julien's white Sanogyl.

A toothbrush, her own.

251

A hairbrush, pig's bristle, belonging to Julien.
A horn comb, her own.
Some cakes of expensive soap, Julien's.
A box of Tampax normal.
A little bottle of powdered kohl given her by her mother.
A little rod made of olive wood, carved by her grandfather in Algeria.
In the inside pockets of the bag, she added:
Her red and black notebooks nicked from a Chinese shop.
Writing paper
Some cassettes, liberally distributed by Krim.
Some books, her portable library: novels by Mohamed Dib and Mouloud Feraoun which she hasn't read yet. *Nedjima, The Repudiation, Algerian Women in their Apartment, Nana*, which she hasn't had time to read. Two books by Rousseau, taken from Julien's collection: *Discourse on the Origin of Inequality* and the *Confessions* and, finally, *Soledad Brother*, the prison letters of George Jackson.
Last of all, on top:
The road map of France.
The road map of Algeria, until such time as she could get hold of ordnance survey maps.

In her shoulder bag, she put:
One red and black notebook.
Envelopes.

252

Stamps.
A Waterman fountain pen given her by Julien.
Waterman cartridges black and violet.
A purse made of beads, given her by her mother.
Her residence permit.
Pieces of chalk, red and white for leaving messages.
Whiting for graffiti on window-panes.
Three lipsticks, Dior *Fury* No. 847, nicked from the perfume counter of a big department store.

She had neither address-book, engagement-book, mascara, rouge, cigarettes – consequently no cigarette-lighter – no photos of Julien or her family, no wallet.

A Puma penknife with lock catch, given her by Krim.

She made a bundle, or rather several, of the clothes she wasn't going to wear, the shoes she wasn't taking with her and anything belonging to her that she didn't want lying about here, and straight away threw the lot into the rubbish chute.

She left a note for Julien asking him to look after her mother's jewellery, he'd find it all in the bookcase behind the books of pictures of *The War in Algeria* or *Rural France* she couldn't remember which and hadn't time to look; at the end of the note which she left open on the desk in the bedroom, she wrote, 'I'll be walking across

253

France as far as Marseilles, and then Algeria. I've got maps, I won't get lost.'

On a page torn out of one of the notebooks in which she kept her diary and wrote her poems which she'd never let anyone read – before she left, she must remember to send a couple to Esther for her magazine for African and West Indian women – Sherazade wrote, 'I love you. S,' She folded the page in eight and slipped it under Julien's pillow. On the mirror in the bathroom, above the washbasin, she wrote with her lipstick, 'I love you. S.' and before she pulled down the plastic shutters, she wrote on one of the window panes with whiting – she always kept a piece in the pocket of her blouson – 'I love you. S.'

She left, slamming the door behind her. She'd left the keys inside.

Matisse

Sherazade spent the day in the library at the
National Centre for Art and Culture, that everyone called Beaubourg and which you could see
picture postcards of everywhere, taken from the
front, the back, the side, the air, by day and by
night. There were even reproductions of the
Centre painted by a third-rate Place du Tertre
artist. These postcards sold better than reproductions of pictures from the National Museum
of Modern Art, that Sherazade hadn't yet visited.
Julien had told her about it. She hadn't got his
habit of going to museums, art galleries. She
liked looking at the posters in the street, in the
Metro, but to stand in front of a picture hung in a
room in an art gallery just to be looked at, in that
particular spot, at a certain time, standing in
front of it, without quite knowing why she
should pay more attention to this picture rather
than that one ... A picture had to move her

deeply, like an image, a photo, a poster. She was certain that if she'd talked to her squat-mates about *The Women of Algiers* in the Louvre, they'd have laughed at her, they'd have called her a bourgeoise or a tourist, she'd have felt insulted, they'd have quarrelled and perhaps she'd never have seen them again. For them, pictures in art galleries represented rotten bourgeois culture, the decadent West, it was old, stale, dead . . . It didn't exist. They lived their lives separate, elsewhere . . . If an art gallery had burnt down, it wouldn't have affected them. They knew, through some of their receiver friends, the value of what people called works of art, and the loadsamoney you could get for them, but for the work itself, they'd no idea and couldn't give a damn. A Picasso, a Renoir, or a Delacroix, stolen from collectors or from galleries, this was just incidental, a means of evaluating the risks and profits of the operation, but as for the object itself, it was just an object. Sherazade didn't tell her squat-mates what she read either. They didn't read much, and then only newspapers, political works, detective stories, and most of all comics that she glanced through when she found them near the red armchair in front of the telly, or in the loo where albums piled up round the pan, you didn't know where to put your feet. Pierrot liked political novels; he knew them all and often talked about them when they all gathered in the kitchen or late into the night when the TV had been switched off. The latest, that Pierrot kept telling them bits of, although he didn't agree with the politics of the blokes who'd written it, was called *Powder Kegs*, Sherazade had begun it but she'd be leaving without being able to finish it. She wouldn't take it with her, it was too heavy to carry.

Julien wouldn't be coming to the library, he'd said he'd be busy all day and late into the evening. Sherazade chose a corner protected by the green shelves, a sort of isolated fortress where she'd be undisturbed till closing time.

When she was walking back through the corridors of the Centre she saw, as she'd always seen without taking any real notice, written on a white board in black letters, ART GALLERY, she didn't hesitate and immediately made her way to the gallery,

Open every day
except Tuesdays
from 12.00h to 22.00h
Saturdays and Sundays
from 10.00h to 22.00h

In her shoulder bag, she'd kept two bars of nut chocolate that she'd picked up at Julien's just before slamming the door.

She was expecting to find rooms enclosed

with ceiling and panelling, high dark walls. She found it was constructed on the principle of a maze of cubicles like the open-plan library up above. Here the walls were white and hard. When you looked up you saw enormous pipes in somewhat neutral colours. The women sitting giving information to the visitors didn't look at all like the attendants at the Louvre. They didn't wear uniforms, simply a badge. Sherazade walked for some time from one cubicle to another, without any landmark except the windows through which you could see Paris and the Sacré Coeur, which she'd never been into but which she knew well from the outside, as she'd had to meet someone there several times about the business of the forged identity card that she still hadn't got. Perhaps Pierrot would surprise her when she went to the squat after leaving the gallery, if he'd got back and hadn't stayed up north for Yasmine. He might have her card and they could leave straight away.

Sherazade sat down facing the big windows, with her back to the pictures which she hadn't looked at, and the gallery far behind her.

She stayed there a long time, as if on a terrace. She thought that what was missing was the sea; but a blue mist behind Paris, if she screwed up her eyes tight for a few seconds, then opened them, was the sea; as she'd never seen it, anything was possible.

She gazed at the sea until evening.

Someone came in. Sherazade heard, 'Is there anyone in there?' She climbed noiselessly on to the lavatory-seat; through the crack at the bottom of the door you could see the feet of the person inside if you looked. No one tried the door. Who would think of shutting themselves in the toilets? You'd have to be mad, and besides, if anyone had been there they'd have answered. Up to now nothing like that had ever happened.

With the emergency exits locked, and no admittance to the museum through the main entrance after ten p.m. except for staff, Sherazade was now alone in the dark in a space that she'd made no attempt to get to know. She had to stay close to the windows to take advantage of the lights of Paris by night. Sherazade ate one of the bars of chocolate, slowly, then got up to go and get a drink of cold water from the washbasin in the toilet. In the most isolated cubicle, the smallest and darkest, she found a spot which suited her.

She fell asleep.

Sherazade never had a watch, but like her grandfather, she knew the time exactly to a couple of minutes. It was seven o'clock when she woke up. The gallery opened at midday.

She washed her face thoroughly in the washbasin, like her father did in the mornings. She rubbed her hands several times over her cheeks, her ears, neck, and blew her nose with water, like the Arabs, and certain fanatical ecologists who do a kind of inhalation with water in the morning to purify themselves from the night and in the evening to get rid of the day's urban pollution. She tidied her hair with her fingers, she didn't feel like opening the big bag and she always forgot to put a pocket comb in her shoulder-bag. Since she'd had her hair cut very short she could pat down the sides and run her fingers through the curls on top and in front to restore their spring. She'd first decided to wear a soft felt hat that Basile had lent her to hide her long hair. But the second or third day she'd gone into a local hairdresser's, the first one she came to, to have her hair cut without really knowing what she was going to ask for. The hairdresser said it was a ruination, when so many women would have given anything for such hair. Sherazade insisted and the hairdresser lifted the mass of soft curly hair, felt the weight expressed his admiration again and what a shame to sacrifice it to a ridiculous fashion that didn't flatter women, he told Sherazade, who was still waiting for him to make up his mind. He asked her if she'd mind giving him her hair. Sherazade agreed immediately to make him get on with it. He called the apprentices and the other hairdressers who gathered round him, adding their exclamations as he cut. Sherazade threw her slides into the wicker basket at her feet.

When she came to pay, the hairdresser said she didn't owe him anything. She'd given him her hair.

Sherazade continued to wear Basile's felt hat and occasionally the dark glasses that Krim lent her since he'd found two other pairs even more 'teriff'.

Sherazade walked through the gallery, munching the rest of the chocolate. She glanced casually at the pictures, without pausing. She reached the foot of the escalator which leads to the fourth floor, where the permanent collections are housed. She went up and walked about on the floor. She found herself passing the same pictures, when she thought she'd got to the opposite end to the spot where she'd started. It must be nine o'clock. She'd plenty of time. She went on walking around. She stopped several times in front of the pictures: after a short time she found herself coming back to the same ones and realized that these pictures that she'd looked at a couple of times, apparently at random, were all portraits of women in various poses and attitudes, but nearly always reclining on a sofa or seated with a book, brunettes, or red-heads, with black or green eyes. Without following any exact order, Sherazade took out her red and black notebook and meticulously copied down the name of the artist, the title and date of each picture as they struck her untrained eye:

Tamara de Lempicka
  Girl in Green (undated).
Moïse Kisling
  Woman in Polish Shawl, 1928.
Suzanne Valadon
  The Blue Bedroom, 1923.
Pierre Bonnard
  The Red Blouse, 1925.
  Woman at her Toilet, 1914.
Picasso
  Woman in Grey, Reading, 1920.
Otto Dix
  Portrait of the Journalist Sylvia von Harden, 1926.
Fernand Léger
  Women in an Interior, 1921.
Balthus
  The Turkish Room, 1963–1966.
Matisse
  Woman Reading, against a Black Background, 1939.

Sherazade wrote Matisse carefully, without thinking. She looks at the picture again and on the label on the right she sees MATISSE. 'Shit! it's Matisse! . . .' She says it aloud, as if she were speaking to someone. She reads again: MATISSE; 'It's Matisse' . . . She looks round, turns the pages of her notebook, this is the first genuine one she's seen. She peers again at the woman reading, from close to. She finds nothing exceptional about her. She even thinks the drawing is a bit awkward. She feels her heart beating faster. That happened with *The Women of Algiers*. Sherazade retraces her steps, tries to proceed in order, doesn't succeed, begins again, looks carefully at each picture, because of Matisse, without yet knowing why Matisse.

She's seen all the pictures in the end rooms and those in the middle, without their making any particular impression. She walks straight ahead, thinking she must have made a mistake ... And then, right in front of her, she sees her, red on a red background. She comes closer, wondering why she hadn't noticed her before – it will soon be twelve o'clock. She is standing in front of the odalisque. First she reads:

Henri Matisse
Le Cateau Cambrésis 1869 – Nice 1954
Odalisque in Red Trousers, 1922
Purchased by the State, 1922
Lux 085 P

Before looking at the picture, she copies into her notebook everything she reads on the little metal plate.

Sherazade is looking at *The Odalisque in Red Trousers*.

She can't understand why it moves her. The reclining woman, with bare breasts, her arms draped in a light gauze behind her head, her hair half hidden by a muslin scarf embroidered with beads, has small round black eyes, a small mouth, almost a double chin – on account of her pose – Sherazade doesn't find her beautiful. The loose red trousers leave her navel exposed. The blouse has slipped to one side revealing her torso and belly. The red trousers are caught in at the calves by a sort of golden yellow band which picks up the colour of the flowers at the bottom of the trousers, yellow and green on the left leg which is folded under her on the almond-green and old-gold striped velvet sofa. The walls around the sofa are covered with tiles, decorated with yellow and red, blue and white, green and white arabesques. On a minute round table, on the right of the reclining odalisque, a vase with three red roses, rather frail. The floor is red, like the trousers.

Sherazade stares at her until midday.

She wrote the description of the odalisque in her notebook without any details, without stating that she thought this woman rather ugly but that she was nevertheless moved by her. She does not try to analyse why.

Her mind is made up. Sherazade will go to Algeria. She no longer hesitates. She'll leave this evening with Pierrot if he's going in the Orleans direction, without Pierrot if he's staying in Paris.

It is twelve o'clock.

Sherazade stopped at the bookshop inside the art gallery and bought all the postcards of the *Odalisque* which remained on the stand. The assistant was astonished.

'You're taking them all. You haven't made a mistake?'

'No.'

'You're sure? I charge you for the ten?'

'Yes.'

'What is it about her that appeals to you?'

'I don't know.'

'She's more beautiful in the original, don't you think?'

'No.'

The assistant held out to Sherazade the envelope with the odalisques.

'Are you perhaps doing a study on Matisse?'

'No, no.'

'I'm curious.'

'That's true. Goodbye.'

The assistant smiled at Sherazade.

Before she left the art gallery and the Centre, Sherazade sent an odalisque to her sister

Meriem. She'd written, 'I'm leaving Paris this evening. Tell them not to look for me. I'm leaving for Algeria. I'm OK, I'll send news.'

Julien

Julien had barely given the door a push. He knew that Sherazade had gone. He'd bought kiwi-fruit, oysters and a passion-fruit sorbet. He'd spent the afternoon at the School of Oriental Languages, translating verses by an Arab woman poet. He wanted to use them as an epigraph for the film of which he'd written the script. They were to start shooting in a fortnight. He was coming to tell Sherazade.

He rubbed the declarations of love off the window and the bathroom mirror.

He went to bed early and unplugged the telephone. He fell asleep without dreaming of Sherazade.

When he stripped his bed to remake it thoroughly, ten or fourteen days after Sherazade's departure, he found the note folded in eight under the pillow.

He hadn't heard from her.

Bagatelle

When she left the art gallery, Sherazade ran all the way to the squat. Pierrot saw her arrive flushed and out of breath. She threw her bag down in the room and flopped into the red armchair. Pierrot followed her. He was alone.

'You're leaving?'

'Yes, I'm leaving. What about you? You said you'd phone on Thursday at twelve o'clock. That's tomorrow. I came back before, that's all.'

'You want to leave today?'

'Yes.'

'What's the hurry? What's got into you? You decide like that, all of a sudden, it's today or never, at a moment's notice, without warning anyone beforehand, and you think people can drop everything for you?'

'I didn't say that. I said I'm leaving today. If you're going in the Orleans direction, you can take me, if not I'll go by myself. I'm not forcing

269

you to leave if you can't.'

'Listen. I've just got back. I've settled everything up north, with the group, with Basile. I'm ready. But I wanted to hang about in Paris for a bit, for no particular reason. I haven't done that for a long time; walking in a garden or a park, it's fine today; I feel I'm living a subterranean existence, even if I don't really work underground, in the Metro or night watchman in the corridors. I feel like going to a quiet garden where they grow beautiful prize flowers for shows, Vincennes, the Bagatelle Gardens, you know them?'

'No. What about Yasmine? You saw her?'

'Yasmine. Yes, I saw her. She's married to a Moroccan, studying in Lille, I think. We went to a café, it's the first time I've ever seen her in a café. We talked. She wants to train to be a youth organizer or probation officer. Her husband will help her. He doesn't insist on her staying at home. He isn't old, he's twenty-seven, the same as me. She seemed happy. I scarcely said a word. It was as if I'd never been in love with her. She was a different person. Her husband came and joined us in the café. We talked about Morocco, the political situation. I gathered he's not allowed to go back there, like a lot of militants who managed to escape from the repression there or who went into voluntary exile after several months in prison. He told me he was militating for the application of Human Rights

270

in Morocco and everywhere where liberty and the rights of the individual are flouted; we didn't see eye to eye, I think his political stance is too soft; it's all right for the West, not for the Third World. You must answer violence with violence. I believe in popular violence. I think it's justified against autocratic violence and state violence. Yasmine's husband said he was going to set up a Committee for the North with some others and he'd be coming to Paris to confer with comrades on the paper *Sans Frontière* to see what joint action was possible. Yasmine will come with him. She's a militant too. Members of her family are in prison in Morocco. I didn't know. After all, we'd talked so little. I shan't see them in Paris. I shall be far away. You coming to Bagatelle? Afterwards we'll leave.'

'Is Bagatelle far?'

'Near the Bois de Boulogne. We'll get straight on to the motorway for Orleans. I've got everything ready. The car's parked down below. You'll see, it's a new one. I'm delighted with it. I've wanted one like it for a long time.'

'You've bought it?'

'There are ways and means . . . You'll see, you'll like it.'

'Oh, you know, me and cars . . . I prefer bikes. I wanted to have a bike before I left. Krim promised me . . . He's still in Japan. Omar's in prison too. So, you see, I don't know when I'll get the bike . . . If I stayed . . . but I'm leaving.'

271

'Shall we go?'

Sherazade hadn't had time to see Zouzou and France before she left, so she wrote them a note on one of the postcards of the *Odalisque*. She told them she was leaving, possibly for a long time, but she'd send them plenty of messages through the independent radio stations and the personal columns of *Libé* or *Sans Frontière* which they'd been reading now and then, since they'd got to know Sherazade. At the end of the note she added, 'It's on account of her that I'm going.' Zouzou and France racked their brains over the meaning of this last sentence without managing to throw light on it. They pinned up the *Odalisque* on a board above their bed, with other postcards they received, one from Tunisia, the other from Martinique, in between palms and coconut trees, the *Odalisque* kept close company with the Caribbean and the South Seas.

At the Bagatelle Gardens Pierrot and Sherazade chat as they walk. Pierrot pauses to read the names of the roses along the paths of the rose-garden. They have royal and aristocratic names he thinks this ridiculous, rather a scream, like a theatre set. The sit down for a moment in the green shelter overlooking the gardens. Pierrot talks about his mother. He's her only son; he told her he was leaving without mentioning his political mission; he gave her to believe he was spending a holiday in the South, he knew she didn't believe him but she didn't ask any questions. When he left, she kissed him affectionately, putting her arms round his neck to bend his face down to hers – he's much taller than her – and saying, 'Pierrot, you are my Pierrot,' like when he was a child, 'come back soon.' She gave him some money, a thousand francs; she knows he hasn't got much; she still does dressmaking at home for friends, neighbours, she's a good worker, she doesn't really need it to live on; she's saving up for a garden she wants to buy near the house and for Pierrot.

Pierrot talks. Sherazade listens.

They have a coffee on the terrace under the trees in the Bagatelle Gardens. It's quiet. They are almost alone at this time of the day. Pierrot has never given any details about his underground activities. Sherazade knows nothing except that he belongs to a secret organization and that he's got some undertaking with Basile who he has to meet in the South or somewhere, he didn't say where. Sherazade thinks it's something to do with arms-smuggling or a hold-up for the group which needs money, since, as Pierrot has always emphasized, they aren't financed by the KGB or the CIA or Libya or international Zionism . . . It doesn't occur to her it could be an Italian-style kidnapping still less a bomb attack. Before they left the squat a little time ago, Pierrot said to Sherazade, 'Open your hands and close your eyes.'

'Why?'

'It's a surprise . . .'

As soon as Pierrot put it in her hand, before she opened her eyes, she guessed it was the .38.

'Why are you giving me this? I don't need it . . .'

'Neither do I.'

'What am I supposed to do with it?'

'I dunno. It may come in useful for someone walking through France like you . . .'

'And if the cops stop me?'

'They won't search you. Put it in your belt, under your T-shirt.'

'Can I chuck it in a ditch when I'm fed up with it?'

'Not on your life . . . A .38's very valuable. You don't realize.'

'It bugs me a bit to have it.'

'Keep it just the same.'

'OK. Shall we go?'

'*Off we go, O, O, . . .*'

'You know that song?'

''Course I know it. I've seen *Pierrot le fou*, you weren't born so you think . . .'

'I know it too . . . Julien often watches it.'

'Who's Julien?'

'A buddy.'

'What's he do?'

'Films, computers, Arabic . . .'

'And you liked *Pierrot le fou*? 'Cause your generation don't understand a thing, it bores them stiff this film, the only thing they like is bloody silly whodunits with Delon and Belmondo, old squares hamming it up . . .'

'I like it when the girl – her name's Marianne, I think – sings "*ma ligne de chance . . . ma ligne de hanche . . .*" and they dance in a pinewood. I also like the part when they're on an island with a parrot, they read all the time, any old thing, I've forgotten.'

Pierrot had taken out the road map for the West and South-West to look up the B roads. He wanted to leave the motorway after Palaiseau, and from Etampes take a secondary road as far as Pithiviers. He'd go through Orleans to see the Loire and because of Joan of Arc, after all, a woman war leader . . . He asked Sherazade what she thought of Joan of Arc, she didn't think anything.

'For the Loire, we'll go as far as Beaugency . . . Orleans, Beaugency, Notre-Dame-de-Cléry, Vendôme, Vendôme . . . it's like a counting-out rhyme.'

Orleans

On the grass, near the terrace of the café in the Bagatelle Gardens, Pierrot spread out the map of Western France and with Sherazade traced the yellow lines of the secondary roads: after Etampes, the D921 as far as Pithiviers, and if they wanted to go through Orleans, the D927 then the D97. After Orleans, where they wouldn't linger or just to have a sandwich with a beer or a Coke, he'd take the D951, going through Cléry in the direction of Beaugency, the D19 as far as the Loire which they'd follow to Tours on the D951 which became the D751 after Blois.

Sherazade asked Pierrot the reason for all these detours. Pierrot, who didn't like Paris – he said so often enough – felt like wandering through France on the by-ways outside the capital, outside Paris, Paris wasn't France. He wanted trees, grass, hedges, streams, rivers, country lanes. That's what he was leaving a day earlier for, to dawdle, to go off the beaten track. In Paris, too, he was a wanderer, but without the freedom of narrow, deserted roads, these gravel roads which still exist and which he loved to drive down with a powerful car raising a cloud of yellow dust behind it. He would stop, get out, set off again, accelerate, braking suddenly with a viciousness that these country roads allowed.

'You've got your walkman, I've got a radio in the car, it's fantastic. Besides, it's lovely weather. It's five o'clock. A good time to get out of Paris and drive like mad or at fifteen miles an hour.'

Pierrot took Sherazade's arm, swung her with him round the clumps of trees in the gardens and ran with her to the car – a grey metallic BMW, a respectable middle-class car, it wouldn't occur to the police to stop him, he was neat, clean-shaven, nothing to find fault with, everything perfect – Pierrot examined Sherazade.

'I'm looking at you to make sure you're not going to compromise me: I'm looking at you through the eyes of a cop: hair, a bit short at the sides, it's the fashion, everyone's used to it, the cops as well, white T-shirt you see them everywhere, it'll do, discreet earrings . . . The scarf, you can keep that on . . . But be sure you don't wear your hat or your dark glasses . . . we'd never even get as far as the motorway . . .'

'And if I feel like wearing them . . .?'

'If you put them on, you leave by yourself, you

277

can hitch, it's not difficult. Look at me, haven't you noticed? I've shaved off my moustache, when after all . . . I know you like wearing disguises, but if you want me to take you, felt hats and pimp's glasses are out . . . Neutral, nondescript . . . Even the leather jacket, you know, *Perfecto* style, stands out, so as long as the sun's shining you leave it on the back seat . . . cool, cool, no provocation . . . You understand . . . no bloody nonsense.'

'OK, OK! Stop your lessons . . .'

'Really, just listen to this . . .'

'If you add another word, I'll hitch . . .'

'What word?'

'You know very well.'

'Yes. OK. Getting in? We'll switch on France Musique. I like France Musique in the car.'

Pierrot and Sherazade are on their way to Pithiviers. Pierrot sings at the top of his voice, turning up the volume on the radio.

'It's Brahms's *Lieder*, you know them?'

'No.'

'Did you know, when he was thirteen he played the piano in German taverns?'

'So what?'

'So, it's the same as us, we'll play in clubs and bars . . . When I come back and Krim too, we'll form a proper group with Basile, you'll see . . .'

'But you're already quite old . . .'

'Not as old as all that, you know. Krim's nineteen, Eddy nineteen or twenty, Basile's twenty-three. I'm the oldest and you're the youngest. You'll sing like Sappho, if you like, or Nina or someone, anyone, they're all old hat all those, Mama Béa as well . . . anyway you'll sing, that's the main thing.'

'Yes, I'll sing. I'll be the singer in the group and I'll be Zina in Julien's friend's film . . . When I get back from Algeria, if I come back. What'll you call your group?'

'We haven't decided . . . The Arabian Nights, you'd like that?'

'No way!'

'Why not?'

'Don't like it . . .'

'Listen. Brahms is beautiful. No one likes him . . .'

'Will you take off those headphones! Really! Can we talk or can't we? We never talk when we're not in a car. Just for once . . . You keep putting them on and I can't stand it. Take them off,' Pierrot repeated.

'No. I can hear quite well.'

'It's not the same . . . I can't talk to you.'

'Too bad!'

'You either take them off or you get out.'

Pierrot brakes. Sherazade opens the door, takes her bag and gets out. Pierrot drives off, Sherazade waves. He can see her in the rear-view mirror. He accelerates. The car disappears.

Sherazade has forgotton her jacket. She walks in the middle of the road. She's put on her dark glasses. She's left her hat on the back seat.

The BMW backs up to Sherazade at full speed. Pierrot brakes, opens the door, throws the hat and the jacket out; he drives off, the tyres shrieking, Sherazade waves. Pierrot can see her in the rearview mirror, he stops, opens the right-hand door. Sherazade doesn't get in, she walks on. Pierrot drives very slowly, keeping level with her.

'Are you going far, mademoiselle?'

'To Orleans.'

'Can I give you a lift, I'm going to Orleans myself. Would you like to get in?'

In Pithiviers Sherazade drank a Coca-Cola and Pierrot several beers while playing the pintables. Sherazade has sat down near the window. She's writing a note to Julien which she won't send, telling him about Matisse and the arabesques of the odalisque. Pierrot has put a record on the juke-box called *Eyes the Colour of Mint*, sung by Eddy Mitchell. Sherazade looks up. Pierrot is looking at her. She was writing to Julien. She takes the letter, tears it up into the ashtray and Pierrot burns it with his lighter – a lighter with Marilyn on that Basile gave him.

Pierrot buys some Gauloises. He doesn't like the Marlboros that the squat-mates smoked.

He's old. It's true he's the oldest. But when they ran out of Marlboros they smoked his Gauloises.

Pierrot has opened out the road map of France on the table near the pin-machine.

'Why do you look at the map all the time? Don't you know it by heart? You know where you're going.'

'I like road maps, that's why. And I've always liked geography.'

Before leaving, Pierrot puts *Eyes the Colour of Mint* on again.

Sherazade didn't want to hang around Orleans. She couldn't give a damn for Joan of Arc and Pierrot didn't insist. He caught sight of her on her horse or on foot, he's not quite sure, that satisfied him.

They drove on towards Beaugency.

Sherazade took off her headphones. 'It's Verdi!' Pierrot said, 'Yes, *La Traviata*, but I prefer his *Requiem*. My father had an Italian friend, a miner who'd come from Lorraine, from Longwy to be exact, who knew nothing but Verdi and listened to nothing else. He couldn't help singing along with the singers. He was our neighbour. I heard Verdi all the time until Aldo's death, his name was Aldo, like Aldo Mori . . . a mine accident.

My father told us about it. My mother didn't want us to go and see, I slipped away but she caught me and had to keep hold of me until my father got back. It was like in Zola and some pictures that I've seen since, reproduced in art magazines, a picture called *The Death of a Worker*; the artist was born in the mines. The death of the Italian who sang Verdi is *The Death of a Worker*, I'd really like to see it one day in the original; when I get back to Paris I'll go and see the artist and ask him to show it me or tell me if it's in an art gallery. If you come back you must go and see it too. *The Death of a Worker*, you'll see, it's really beautiful. The story of Aldo and the picture of the worker who died like Aldo really upset me. My father cried when he told me about it. We all went to the funeral. The municipal orchestra played Verdi. Because of him, the whole mine and the whole town sang Verdi. Even the children.'

Before they got to the Loire, Pierrot had insisted on driving round Beaugency. He remarked to Sherazade that she was in a little French town, really French, such as she'd not see anywhere else.

'Look at it, Sherazade, look closely.'
'It won't disappear . . . What's got into you?'
'I love France . . .'
'Are you off your rocker or what?'

'Not at all. I can say I love France, can't I? To you . . . because the buddies . . . they couldn't give a damn . . . so, I love France.'

'You talk as if we were going to die.'

'You think so?'

Pierrot pulled up in front of the statue of Joan of Arc. He'd expected to see her in Orleans, he sees her in Beaugency, standing carrying her banner. Her sword has lost its blade but the sheath lies against Joan's thigh, through the coat of mail over the folds of her skirt her spiked knee-guards can be seen. The warrior Joan resembles a woman, with large rounded hips . . . For once, Pierrot thinks. 'That's Joan of Arc.'

'So I see.'

Pierrot reached the bottom of the hill, near the square shaded by lime-trees.

They were listening to Verdi. Pierrot said 'You can smell the Loire' and Sherazade 'What if we drove across the Loire?' . . . 'In the car?' 'Yes, in the car, of course' Sherazade said with a laugh. Pierrot stared at her, said 'You bet' and gripped the steering-wheel like a stunt-man, 'Hold tight Sherazade, look out, we're crossing the Loire, shut your eyes, we're across . . .'

Sherazade was laughing. Pierrot put his foot down hard on the accelerator. The Loire was in front of them.

The little road that runs beside the Loire leading nowhere, the Rue de l'Abbaye, is lined with plane-trees. A house with green shutters on one side and a few yards away, on the other side, a bench above a terrace which slopes down to the river. Pierrot accelerated. The BMW shot through the plane-trees, hit the bench, turned over several times, righted itself on the raised strip of ground, rolled a few yards to the right, and stopped.

Pierrot, still clutching the steering-wheel, didn't move.

Verdi could be heard on the radio.

Sherazade opened her eyes . . . She wasn't hurt. Neither was Pierrot. She shook the door open and jumped out, picked up her bag and hurled it against a plane tree. She'd put on her jacket an hour ago as it began to get cool. She still had her walkman on.

Pierrot hadn't stirred. 'What's the silly bugger waiting for? What the hell's he up to?' Sherazade could see his fair curly hair on the wheel, nothing more. 'What's he buggering about for? Shit!' She ran towards the car door, shouting 'Pierrot! Pierrot!'

On the radio, Callas was singing Verdi.

Sherazade gave a start. It struck her – this shitty Verdi . . . Pierrot can't hear anything when I call him – she saw the smoke before hearing the sound, 'Pierrot! Pierrot! . . .'

She just had time to jump clear. The car blew up. Sherazade recoiled, covering her head. There were more and more explosions, sending the BMW into the air. There was no sign of Pierrot. Sherazade tried to get nearer. Red flames were shooting up. They nearly reached the highest branches of the trees. Dense black smoke enveloped the house with the green shutters. The bench had gone up in flames.

Sherazade leaned against the tree, rooted to the ground, screaming, 'Pierrot! Pierrot! Pierrot! . . .'

The sound of a siren could be heard. When the police arrived, Sherazade had disappeared. They couldn't identify the body. They found traces of arms and explosives. A few yards away, near the Loire, one of the policeman, who'd continued his search as far as the boat that had been moored there for months, discovered bits of the number plate of the stolen car and a scrap of red thread. 'He was with a woman,' the policeman thought. 'She must have copped it too.'